9.95

LR644

LR267

Books should be returned or renewed by the
last date stamped above

**KENT
ARTS &
LIBRARIES**

OPEN ACCESS

**Kent
County
Council**

ARTS & LIBRARIES

VENETIAN SPRING

Sonia Phillips

In the scintillating Venice of sparkling canals and marble palaces, Carrie met Tristano Cavalli, the wealthy heir of an aristocratic Italian family. She fell head over heels in love with him, and hoped that he was in love with her. She was aware of his reputation for being a playboy, and she was determined not to fall prey to his charm. When their very different ideas about life and morality clashed, their meetings produced more sparks than stars.

VENETIAN SPRING

Sonia Phillips

Curley Publishing, Inc.
South Yarmouth, Ma.

Library of Congress Cataloging-in-Publication Data

Phillips, Sonia.
  Venetian spring / Sonia Phillips.
    p. cm.
  1. Large type books.   I. Title.
  [PS3566.H518V46   1992]
  813'.54—dc20
  ISBN 0–7927–1247–1 (hardcover)   91–43487
  ISBN 0–7927–1248–X (softcover)   CIP

Published in Large Print by arrangement with Donald MacCampbell, Inc. in the United States, Canada, the U.K. and British Commonwealth and the rest of the world market.

Distributed in Great Britain, Ireland and the Commonwealth by CHIVERS PRESS LIMITED, Bath BA2 3AX, England.

Printed in Great Britain

VENETIAN SPRING

CHAPTER 1

In a few minutes the plane would touch down in Italy!

Even now Carrie wanted to pinch herself to make sure this was real. When Ed Stern asked her to accompany him on a business trip to Venice, she was plunged in momentary panic. To visit such a fabled city filled her both with delight and horror. What could she wear? European elegance was not her style though she knew blue jeans and cotton tops would not be acceptable for such a prestigious company venture. With her sister Amy's help she embarked on a whirlwind shopping spree from which she embarked reasonably well equipped in knit garments her sister assured her could be drip-dried over the tub each night to emerge sparkling fresh in the morning. When Carrie joined Stern and Associates last fall she never dreamed of such an adventure, nor would she, the lowliest secretary, normally have been chosen for this assignment had Eve not been on vacation, the other secretary deeply involved in a hot business deal in Texas.

"Fasten all seat belts."

1

Carrie checked her appearance in her mirror as the stewardess made the announcement before they briefly touched down at Rome's Leonardo da Vinci International Airport. In a pale oval face surmounted by bouncy coppery waves, wide spaced green eyes stared back. Amy had persuaded her to try a new makeup program to go with the more sophisticated clothes; formerly a 'lipstick only' girl, Carrie was pleased by the glamorous changes, eye shadow, blusher and mascara brought about. Her nose was narrower, her eyes smokily enlarged. It was not hard to believe her sister's laughing promise romance awaited her once she stepped on Italian soil.

From across the aisle Ed Stern grinned in reassurance, aware of her building excitement easily betrayed by her eager flushed face. Carrie smiled back, taking a deep breath in an effort to overcome the nervous butterflies in her stomach.

Beside her Tim Bryant folded his trade journal and reached for his sweater. Though the young designer had shared her seat on this trans-Atlantic flight, she might as well have been alone, for all the attention he paid her. Shy, always at a loss for words, Tim was definitely not the heartthrob variety, though from the maneuvering when they boarded, Carrie suspected Ed purposely placed them

2

together in hopes of sparking a romance.

Tim could only be described as colourless; a classification too many of her former boyfriends shared. All through college Mother carefully schooled her to stay away from the wilder males, nudging her towards the acceptable young men in their church group on whom she beamed approval, remarking favorably on their shortish hair and neat clothing. While Carrie knew she was not experienced enough to manage the most popular boy in school, she enjoyed the fantasy of being swept off her feet by a handsome male who could choose any woman he wished, but settled for her in repetition of all the best late shows filmed during Hollywood's heyday. With a smile she closed her eyes, picturing the make believe scene where she was masterfully dominated by a latter-day Clark Gable. Well, she was certainly going to the right place for that if what she read was to be believed; Italian men professed to be the last holdouts of rugged male dominance.

The deafening noise stopped, the motion ceased; they were in Rome. This exciting discovery erased the shadowy figure from her mind as Carrie prepared to view the foreign sights if only from the airport terminal. This was the first time she had been on a jetliner; the first time she had ventured far from her

3

native Oklahoma. This flight was symbolic of a new beginning worlds away from the tree shaded town with its white frame homes surrounded by neat, clipped lawns where she grew up; far from the pseudo-sophistication of Tulsa, where she now shared an apartment with her girl friend. This was to be her first taste of international living jet age style. And she could hardly wait to begin.

Still feeling as if she was in a dream, Carrie admired the archaic buildings from the hotel window. To think she was in Venice! All those famous landmarks she had read about glistened in the clear bright sun like a book of art prints come alive. Even the hotel, where she had spent a restful night in this huge elaborate bed, appeared to be a former Renaissance palace, while close at hand was the famed Rialto Bridge.

Sparkling in the luminous Canaletto morning the Grand Canal wound between weathered faces of *Palazzos* growing from the water. The raucous voices of gondoliers and venders plying their trade drifted to her window. Red and white striped barber poles jutted from the water at the landing stage below, serving as moorings for the boats which jammed the canal. Mounds of brightly colored produce in open topped crates wove between slow moving gondolas as motorboats sped to market.

So eager to see this fabulous city of literature had she been, Carrie had risen early to absorb her colorful surroundings before Ed Stern called her to work.

Tearing herself from the bobbing vista, from the sparkling water which dazzled her eyes in the sunlight, Carrie admired anew her hotel room with its lofty ceilings patterned in molded leaf design above a gilded surround which seemed twenty feet high, as did the blue satin draperies on the canopied bed. Luxury marked the room, making her wonder what the expenses were per day at this grand establishment which was a far cry from the shoe box sameness of the orange and green decor at the Country Motel where she stayed with her mother when they had visited Dallas.

Knowing her business associates would soon be knocking at her door, Carrie was spurred to action. Despite the brilliant sunlight, the morning air was cool, so she chose a pink striped knit dress and jacket, her favorite among her purchases. Makeup on, her short hairstyle flicked artfully in place, she glanced in the gilded mirror to make sure this really was Carrie Neal. Last night on the water taxi the young Italian boatman had eyed her speculatively, appreciation plain in his expressive dark eyes. His unabashed scrutiny sent shivers down her spine. No man had ever looked at her like that before, those expressions reserved for her heroines of romantic novels.

After a continental breakfast of coffee, rolls and preserves enjoyed in the gilded dining room amid banks of exotic flowers, the three representatives of Stern and Associates, Architectural Consultants, boarded the water taxi to the Banco Cavalli for an interview with their first prospective client.

Tim Bryant was more friendly this morning. Even he appreciated the vast improvement in Carrie's appearance as he gallantly steadied her arm when the surging craft took off.

"Hi, I wouldn't have known you decked out like that," he said with a toothy smile. "How are you enjoying the trip?"

"Fine. This is such a fantastic place," she enthused, absorbing the exotic scene of flapping red and blue sun awnings and gondoliers in red banded straw hats poling their crafts over the glittering water.

Pulling a face, Tim glanced about with jaded eye. "It's different all right. Do you know, I couldn't get one stick of gum in the entire hotel. Luxury hotel they might call it, but I could smell this canal all night. What they need is a good air conditioning unit to cut out the smell."

His remark put a damper on Carrie's enthusiasm. Now as they sped through the ripples she became uncomfortably aware of the rising odor of drains, of tainted mud, and other unspeakable smells mingled in the oily slick at the shallows of the canal.

"Don't let the old pessimist spoil your fun," Ed laughed, lighting his pipe. "Venice is not to be measured by drains and a plastic economy."

Hearing the unspoken rebuke in Ed's words, Tim grinned sheepishly. His turned-up nose sprinkled with freckles added boyish vulnerability to his face. Though only in his twenties, his expanding waistline belted unflatteringly with a white vinyl belt slicing deeply into his navy knit pants and shirt, suggested premature middle-age.

"I think Venice is romantic and so much different from home, it's like another world," Carrie pronounced emphatically, breathing a sigh of pleasure at the sheer color of the sparkling scene spreading about her.

"What's wrong with home?" Tim demanded. "Our country's the best, the leader in everything."

"For heaven's sake don't say that to an Italian," Ed chuckled, tapping his pipe against

7

the rail. "I'd hate to have to rescue you from a screaming mob."

The smug smile froze on Tim's face and he cleared his throat. "Don't you agree with me?"

"Oh, Tim, shut up and enjoy the view," Carrie dismissed impatiently, wanting to tell him what she thought of his attitude but knowing this was not the place. "Some people spend their life savings to see this, while here you are getting an expense paid trip and still grumbling. Enjoy it, or at least fake it, so I can enjoy it myself."

The blush spread to Tim's hairline, disappearing in the receeding lanky brown hair and Carrie was satisfied her words had hit home.

"Well said," Ed agreed, secretly applauding Carrie for saying what he had thought, but had not voiced.

Tim was still withdrawn into his shell, wounded by their criticism, when they disembarked to walk the short distance to the bank for their rendezvous with their Italian client.

The Banco Cavalli was ablaze with pink marble, the arched entrance supported by twisted columns. White marble statues were set in niches along the wall of the corridor. Their feet echoed loudly in the vastness

8

making Carrie want to tiptoe; so aware was she of their steps, it was almost like walking in church. Seeing the nude figures in their alcoves, Tim maneuvered positions in order to shield Carrie from the disturbing sight, betraying his puritanical small town upbringing by his behavior.

In a high-ceilinged room overlooking the water they waited around an immense flower inlaid table for *Signor* Cavalli. Interesting stone ornamentation of the balcony drew Tim outside for a closer examination.

"If it were up to him he'd put a MacDonald's in the center of St. Mark's square," Carrie hissed.

"I wouldn't go that far, but Tim certainly is hung up on modern functionality. Wait, he's a real Jekyll and Hyde when he gets pencil and paper in his hand. And modern design is just what this Italian wants for his hotels. He'll like Tim's work."

A few minutes later when *Signor* Cavalli walked briskly inside the room, Carrie forgot about Tim, about everything but that wide shouldered, dark haired, six foot frame of masculinity. Carrie was delighted, yet uncomfortable to be the object of his scrutiny when her pencil plopped to the floor attracting his attention.

Liquid brown eyes washed over her figure,

9

coming to rest on her face in an all encompassing stare which lasted no more than a moment, yet felt as if it was an eternity. A smile began in the eyes long before it curved his well defined lips.

"*Buon giorno, bellissima Signorina,*" he said, his voice low and huskily appraising.

Flustered by his bold gaze, Carrie replied and while the *signore* greeted Ed and Tim she stooped to retrieve her pencil. New to this game of such open masculine appreciation Carrie needed more time to practice her responses yet, as she watched him, head down over Tim's sketches, she was sure years of practise would not have prepared her for a man like *Signor* Cavalli.

She made notes of his preferences, flustered when he sometimes lapsed into Italian. Having his soft brown eyes upon her, seeing that half smile on his lean, olive-skinned face, made the blood surge to her cheeks. He was the most handsome, alluring man she had ever set eyes on. His lithe, athletic build was suited to perfection in well-cut camel gaberdine, a white silk shirt contrasting with the sun tanned sweep of firm jawline. His tie was chocolate brown flecked with silk flowers and he nervously slackened the knot at his neck, drawing her attention to his long, slender brown hands adorned with two gold rings winking fire in the sun from a crescent of rainbow diamonds.

Head in a whirl, Carrie found all too soon the discussion of hotel design was at an end. Ed was shaking his hand while the Italian invited them to visit his villa, leaving Carrie in the background where she tried to appear sophisticated and felt she failed miserably.

"I insist, if we are to be partners, you must not call me *Signor* Cavalli. Tristano is my name."

In a daze Carrie mused how suitably romantic it was then, to her surprise. She found he was speaking to her, his dark eyes quizzical as she continued to stare.

"Sorry, I didn't catch that," she managed, her tongue feeling like a wad of Kleenex.

"Will you honor me also with your presence *Signorina?*" he asked politely, formal now he addressed her directly, yet not without the trace of sensual approval in his brown eyes.

"I'd love to see your villa. Everything about Venice is fascinating," she managed, smiling, wishing she could turn off her absurd blush at will.

"Well, the villa's about forty miles outside Venice, but if you're fascinated by this decadent beauty, I'll escort you round our *palazzo*. This week we pack everything to leave for the summer. It's your last chance to see it."

"Great, but perhaps Ed . . ."

"No, there's no hurry, you can type the notes later. I want to show Tim the other bank we designed for *Signor* Cavalli, so we won't need you if you want to go sightseeing. Be careful, you know the bad reputation these Latin playboys have."

Carrie watched the Italian's face light in a smile as he winked at Ed. "Ah, yes, must we provide a chaperone?"

"You must be kidding! I'm certainly old enough to look after myself," Carrie blurted, annoyed Ed should draw attention to her lack of sophistication, especially when she was trying to create a whole new image. Now this fantastic man would think she was a dumb little small town girl who had barely been out of her own back yard.

"You don't know Tristano," Ed dismissed. "You mustn't read the gossip columns. If it wasn't for him they'd have to find someone else to speculate about. 'Scion of a wealthy family, the most eligible bachelor in northern Italy was seen wining and dining the beautiful Lady Fotherington Millinghome at an exclusive London club before jetting to his Riviera retreat' . . ."

"How intriguing," Carrie interrupted,

turning to the Italian. "Now I wouldn't miss that tour for the world."

Surprised by her easy boldness, Carrie walked, head high, along the narrow red carpet bisecting the vast marble floor of the *banco's* main lobby.

The Cavalli *Palazzo* was a magnificent assemblage of decorative stonework in multiple balconied archways, of pillars surmounted by gargoyles: the weathered facade, washed by the ebbing canal, mellowed by centuries of sun and rain, reeked with antiquity.

"Do you like it? By the way, I don't know your name. I can't go on calling you *bellissima Signorina*, however true it may be," he said huskily, his breath hot on her neck.

Terribly aware of his presence, not touching her, yet barely whispering across her clothing, Carrie forced a casual smile to her mouth. "My name's Carrie Neal."

"Carrie? What's that short for?"

"Caroline Margaret to be exact."

"Charming. And old fashioned. Are you old fashioned to match?" he asked, reaching around her to pull a bell rope.

Not sure of his meaning, for one glance at his dark face told her it was not merely a casual question, Carrie said, "That depends

13

on what you call old fashioned." She was relieved to find the door being opened, thus diverting his attention. Prepared to flirt with him if that was the game he played, Carrie doubted if her previous experience qualified her for a man like this. Those glamorous faces in the movie magazines were as remote as beings from another planet, yet if Ed's joking warning was to be believed this man moved in those hallowed circles.

A maid admitted them, exchanging greetings in Italian with her master, sparing no more than a brief glance in Carrie's direction.

"That's Maria – she's been with us for years," he explained, ushering his guest through the frescoed entrance court, too rapidly for Carrie who wanted to absorb the unusual beauty of this Renaissance palace in its entirety.

"This is the boatyard, so to speak," he informed, encompassing the tiled area with a nonchalant wave. "Here the gondolas were stored in winter months. At one time my family were merchants, so here too they kept their bales of cloth. The real house begins through here."

"Just a boathouse," Carrie gasped, "but surely those frescoes are valuable."

He glanced over the faded scenes with

14

practiced eye. "Not really. The ancestor who commissioned those hired a bargain painter, not very talented from the art world's standpoint. At one time the outside of the *palazzo* was painted with scenes from mythology, but it was covered with whitewash to rid the building of plague germs."

"What a crime! Didn't they value art?"

"Certainly, but they valued life more," he added with a grin as he ushered her through a recessed doorway. "This is the *mezzanino*, the business part of the house."

The tour continued briskly past offices, through a second doorway, up a second flight of stairs till they came to a beautifully appointed room resplendant with crystal chandeliers and antique furnishings.

"This is the major apartment of the *palazzo*, the *piano signorile*. There's a balcony overlooking the canal if you want to see the view."

The window opened onto a wide stone balcony, the top portion shielded by a honeycomb design of stone through which Carrie saw the teaming ribbon of the Grand Canal. This was the elaborate architecture she had admired from the water. She imagined herself a Renaissance noblewoman, her handsome lover beside her, looking out on a scene familiar even in those days. The

15

dream was terminated by the pleasant warmth of his hand resting lightly on her shoulder, the contact sending tremors of pleasure through her body.

"Beautiful, isn't it," he breathed. "The decadent old lady's about to sink into the sea, yet everything about Venice seems so timeless, so indestructible, I find that hard to believe. My ancestors have lived on this site since the middle ages. The knowledge gives me a strange sense of destiny."

Carrie turned to see his face in shadow, dappled sun lighting his suit with gold, making his hair dark by contrast. His head proudly turned towards the ancient waterways, Carrie was struck by the chiseled appearance of his features. His sensual, generous mouth, the high-bridged nose, the cheekbones prominent beneath the lean, tanned expanse of flesh, all reminding her of a beautiful statue. The dark brows forming a straight line above deep brown eyes added a brooding aura of mystery to his face, as if he hid dark secrets. There was bursting masculinity to those features which, while not coarse, had an overwhelming sense of strength, that same mingled beauty and brutality found in portraits of men of the era when this *palazzo* was built. Tristano Cavalli reflected centuries of force, determination and

16

treachery, character traits which molded his ancestors.

"We have a growing fund to save the city. I'm sure you've heard of it – we get contributions from all over the States."

"Oh yes, there's been a lot of publicity in the press, especially during that flood a few years back."

He smiled. "It floods every spring. We have boards laid across the *piazza* so a person can walk without drowning. Come, enough gloom, let's go indoors."

Once more the light touch of his hand and Carrie felt her blood thrill. In her vivid imagination she magnified that touch to an embrace, to kisses while clasped in his arms, pressed close against the length of his hard frame. Adored, worshipped, he would tell her she was beautiful, how much he loved her – she glanced up to find him eyeing her with quizzical expression. And though he could not know the intimacy of her thoughts, Carrie found blood flame to her cheeks.

"Would you like a cool drink? Lemonade?"

"That'll be fine."

He was gone only a couple of minutes, during which time Carrie admired the luxurious silk paneled walls and glittering crystal chandeliers with awe. And she also tried to repress her unashamedly romantic

17

thoughts. What an idiot! She had not known the man over a couple of hours and she was already picturing them together in the best love scene Hollywood had to offer. It was not entirely her fault, Tristano Cavalli obviously had that effect on other females, hence the avid copy in the gossip magazines. There was too much knowledge in those hot dark eyes, too much the expert in his swift appraisal of her figure to think he was not used to the open admiration of women; admiration he generously reciprocated. But one glance at his sensual face told her he was what Ed suggested; a playboy. A few days of pleasure, a week, then he would move on leaving a trail of broken hearts in his wake. She was determined hers would not be counted amongst them. Handsome he might be, but he had the typical arrogance of his type, bursting with confidence over his ability to enslave any likely female who came within striking distance.

When he returned with tall iced glasses of lemonade, a slice of lemon swirled over the rim of the glass, Carrie had regained what she hoped was enough composure to see her through the day.

"Great," she commented, drawing a long cool sip through a straw.

"Why did you come with *Signor* Stern? He

doesn't need a secretary, especially one who doesn't speak Italian."

"How do you know I don't speak Italian?"

"Do you?"

"Well, no, but I don't think you should assume something right off the bat without even bothering to find out."

He sighed in exasperation. "As I said, why are you here?"

Taken back by his manner, by the long stare from those dark eyes, Carrie spluttered. "Well, I've got notes to type. If Mr. Stern says he needs a secretary, you can bet he does."

"Bah, notes, a sop, no more. They didn't need those." Leaning forward, Tristano viewed her with a speculative smile. "Now I know I'm probably wrong, but – how shall I say it in English – this morning I thought you were Stern's mistress."

In the vast silent room Carrie's gasp sounded like an explosion. At her reaction Tristano chuckled. Placing his empty glass on a marble topped table he crossed to the sunny window awaiting her further comment.

"Ed Stern's happily married," she exploded indignantly, "besides, I'm not *that* kind of girl."

He half turned with a scornful smile. "Oh, and how do you know what *that* kind of

19

girl is like? You surprise me. I thought all American girls were totally 'liberated', as they charmingly put it. You even sound shocked. I'm sorry if I offended you. What part of America do you come from?"

Swallowing indignation, Carrie glared at him, seeing the humor flicker in his face. "Oklahoma, right in the middle of the country."

"Ah, like cowboys, Indians and oil wells, or so I should imagine."

"Where do you get your information from, *Signor* Cavalli? There are no cowboys for miles. In Tulsa we even have a few mini-skyscrapers."

"Amazing! He grinned, barely containing his humor. "Is everyone so morally up-standing there?"

Squashing her irritation, Carrie managed a smile. "I'd hardly say that."

He laughed. "My assumption was a natural one, how was I to know you had such quaint ideas to match your name. Men hardly ever bring their wives to Venice. Stern's been here before, but always alone. You must forgive me." He glanced sideways at her to see the effect of his words, nonplussed by her attitude.

Carrie forced composure, knowing the Italian in him accepted the role of mistress without surprise. It was that superior, arrogant air he assumed which annoyed her so much, yet perhaps it was because she chose to battle with him that his sarcasm was aroused. Men like Tristano Cavalli did not like to be crossed.

"Maybe it's because it's the first time I've been accused of being that."

"Ah, but if you continue to travel with middle-aged men, it won't be the last for someone of your beauty," he assured smoothly, turning back to the sunlit view.

Her beauty! Carrie clasped her sweating palms. Though she should have been insulted by his suggestion, prickles of excitement played along her spine to think he pictured her as one of those worldly women who accompanied their bosses to romantic hideaways. She would hardly class herself as a *femme fatale*, yet if a sophisticated man like Tristano Cavalli found her attractive enough for such a role, he must not think of her as a small town girl at all. His viewpoint also disclosed the different plains of society in which they moved. To the Jet Set such casual affairs were commonplace amusements; to a girl raised in the rigid morality of Elm Heights Baptist Church they remained forbidden scandals.

He stood etched against the brightness,

21

his broad shouldered, slim-hipped figure reminding her of the surprising response created by his touch. How easy it would be to love him; how wonderful to be loved by him.

"So you're not entangled with any man?"

"Not yet."

"You're wise. Too many pretty girls fall for the first man who finds them attractive. After a brief affair they're bitter and disillusioned."

"I'm going to give you hysterics by confessing I don't approve of 'affairs', as you put it, despite what you might think about American girls. We aren't *all* that easy to possess." Though he would never know it, Carrie gulped to learn the accuracy of his observation, how close he had come to discribing the very feeling worming its way into her heart.

"Ha!" he dismissed in scorn. "That must be the fault of American men. Any Italian male would regard you as an intriguing challenge."

"Oh, would he," she snapped, coloring at his mocking tone. Anger making her reckless, she added. "After that sporting statement, I'd be surprised if you aren't entangled with several women at once so anxious are you to save us from emotional deprivation."

"Armed with the knowledge I'm 'the most eligible bachelor in northern Italy', you shouldn't be surprised," he countered

22

sarcastically, turning from the window.

"How stupid of me to overlook that flattering quotation."

When he walked slowly towards her Carrie was struck by the grace of his unhurried movements reminding her of a sleek panther on the prowl. And though his arrogance infuriated her, she must admit he was very appealing.

"Yes, it was, wasn't it? But from a lady of such high moral integrity, hardly surprising."

He stood before her and Carrie lowered her gaze to the flowered brown tie. His eyes said something she did not understand, something which both thrilled and alarmed her at the same time. His hand lightly caressing her hair brought her eyes on a level with him. Admiration, and that other more potent emotion flickered there, drawing her to him when she should have told him to keep his hands to himself, as angry as she felt over his condescending attitude. The reaction was bewildering.

"There have been many women in my past, there are several in the present, but I've never known one quite like you, Carrie." His husky voice throbbed with emotion. "Such naivete is a refreshing change."

"Sorry to disappoint you, but I'm not an emotional wasteland pining to be conquered,"

23

she informed scathingly, green eyes flashing. She had never been so irritated, yet at the same time so attracted to a man before in her life. She should thrust away his caressing hand, yet seemed unable to make the effort so alien to her wants.

Ignoring her angry remark, he grinned with interest at the flashing display of temper. "I admire women with spirit, it makes the pursuit more challenging."

"There'll be no pursuit."

"You have not learned yet one should never dismiss a man totally, you allow him to toy with the prospect of a conquest."

The husky voice, the heavy, emotion charged atmosphere combined to make Carrie feel suffocated by his nearness. He did not touch her hair now, lightly brushing her cheek instead, tracing his lean brown fingers along the soft curve of her face till he reached her chin which he tilted gently upward. Standing close, he smiled down into her flushed face, his expression softening, his brown eyes turning to liquid hue.

"Must we fight? Is this the way of it in your country? I far prefer sparks of another nature. If I promise not to carry you off by moonlight, I wonder if you'll come to a party with me tomorrow night?"

"By then we'll probably be on a plane

for home," she murmured, growing terribly conscious of his nearness, of the burning brand of his fingers lightly touching her face.

"Now that I won't allow. If I must invent a problem to hold your associates here a few more days, I'll do it to assure you of pleasant memories of Venice."

"Would you go that far to keep me here?"

He removed his hand from her face, instantly breaking the spell. "When I want something I use every method available to get it," he assured, stepping back. "Now, shall I return you to the safety of your companions – or do you trust me to take you on a tour of the city?"

Once more the flicker of sarcasm and Carrie's temper rose. "Oh, I'm sure I'll be safe in the daylight."

The too plastic smile of goodwill flashed at her remark was to mask that other emotion she had seen blazing a moment in his dark face. Hard pressed to identify the change, Carrie must call it ruthlessness for want of a better name, that force which turned the brown eyes piercing hard, tautening his jaw, his mouth. Excitement fluttered her heart when she reviewed the implication behind his words, 'when I want something'. Did he want to win her affection, or was that foolish conceit on her behalf? He was the

25

most fascinating, attractive and infuriating man she had ever met. One minute she was prepared to stalk out of here in anger, the next she nearly succumbed to the warmth of his touch. Despite the outward appearance of being in complete control, Carrie knew she must not allow herself to be blind to the danger of such a friendship. However much it roused his anger, she was determined to make him understand she would not become another easy conquest.

CHAPTER 2

The vast *Piazza* of St. Mark was exactly as Carrie had it pictured. Pigeons strutted arrogantly about the flagstones awaiting offerings from the visitors, scattering with agility when handfuls of grain bounced before them. Tourists, thronged only in their hundreds at this time of year, waited at the base of the clock for the hour to strike so they could watch the Moors complete their ritual.

People and pigeons perched side by side on the steps where tourists wrote endless postcards, some even sketching the famous square. Carrie filled out her own share of postcards, while Tristano waited indulgently at the cafe table where they stopped for refreshment. On the north and south of the *piazza* outdoor cafes spread their chairs, commanding a perfect view of the vast patterned floor with its mingled occupants.

"Come, it's almost time for the clock," Tristano said, ushering her towards the appointed place. "In high summer you've got to get here before the half hour to find a spot."

A knot of tourists in drip-dry cottons, wearing dark glasses, open guide books at the ready, watched two bronze moors strike the hours. Exclamations, sighs of pleasure for one more event struck from the list, they moved to the next attraction.

Tristano eyed the departing throng with jaded eye, repeating the sometimes philosophy of many Venetians. "Without them we'd be finished, but God, sometimes I hate them for their pop-eyed stupidity. For only a few is the timelessness of these antiquities of any value. Too many came merely because it's the thing to do."

"Isn't that true of tourists around the world?"

His irritation dissolved in a smile. "Yes. You, no doubt, have your share of Italian families staring openmouthed at all the sights. May God preserve us from tourists."

Tristano purchased a bag of grain. Carrie laughingly threw handfuls of feed to the greedy pigeons, wary when they became airborne, not anxious to be decorated out of affection by these noisy fixtures of the *piazza*.

When they rested at Florian's, sipping tall, coffee flavored drinks, Carrie felt a return of the growing intimacy which had begun after their prickly exchange in the grand salon of *Palazzo* Cavalli.

"I wouldn't have missed today for the world," he said, "even the heated exchanged of ideas." Here he winked and his hand stole across the painted table to rest within inches of her own. "Too bad I can't invite you to dine with me tonight, but I've a previous engagement. The lady would not understand."

Disappointment and annoyance at being taken for granted niggled at her goodwill. Yet Carrie must admit, secretly she had hoped he would monopolize her time for the rest of the day. "Ed and Tim expect me to eat with them," she informed lightly, trying to hide the emotion she was experiencing as she sipped her drink.

"Tomorrow we'll drive to the villa. The Prince and Principessa di Monde own the adjoining property. Your boss intends to design a luxury hotel around their villa if he

28

can sway them to the idea. That could mean we'll be seeing quite a lot of each other."

Carrie recalled the di Monde name being mentioned in Ed's recounting of their clients, but she had not known they were a prince and princess, nor that their property joined that of the Cavallis. Though she did not want to return so soon, she almost wished the plans would fall through, for Carrie was afraid of getting in over her depths with this man. Though she absolutely rejected everything he stood for, she could not help being drawn, despite herself, to accept him for what he was.

"I didn't know we were doing business with royalty," she said, stirring the remnants of her drink.

"We have royalty at every streetcorner. It was only in the last century Italy became a unified nation. Every little sector had its dukes and counts. Half Italy was royal blood, or so they say."

She smiled and looked away, knowing what he implied with his knowing smile; he was probably right, the nobility were famous for their amorous adventures. "Do you think that way of life was right?"

He shrugged. "It must have been great fun."

"Oh, don't you ever take things seriously?" she exploded.

"Not if I can help it."

Carrie glared at him for a moment, then they both burst out laughing. "You're impossible!"

"That's half my charm. Anyway, to change the subject, we won't be able to stay late at the villa because the party's here. You'll like the Santi *Palazzo*, it's one of the most luxurious along the Grand Canal."

"I'd love to come, but I really don't have anything to wear. Is it formal?" Mentally Carrie reviewed her limited wardrobe which had not been assembled to cover grand balls. The ecru dress with the crochet lace banding was the only party attire she had brought.

"Formal – Gabriella's parties are any way you want them to be. This is in aid of the Save Venice Fund. Vast donations are expected. There'll be film stars, a diplomat or two, yes, perhaps you'll find it formal. Many will be in fancy dress, but don't let that worry you, just as many won't."

The mention in such warm tones of a woman named Gabriella brought Carrie's elation crashing down. There was something about the way Tristano spoke her name, that special smile making her think there was more than usual friendship between them. She wanted to ask if he counted the mysterious Gabriella amongst the women of his past, or if she was very much in the present. She wanted to ask, but Carrie knew she had no right. Tristano Cavalli had promised nothing beyond an invitation to a party.

During the sightseeing afternoon around the Doge's Palace, St. Mark's Basilica, even in the square, Carrie was terribly aware of his presence. It disturbed her to find his hand inches from her own, to watch those restless brown fingers with the sparkling rings. She willed him to touch her, then immediately dismissed the thought as foolish. He was probably sitting there planning his battle campaign of how to lure such a simple little victim to his ultimate conquest.

"You've turned so quiet, am I boring you?" he asked, lazily smiling into her eyes. He had such a disconcerting habit of fixing her gaze until she was compelled to look away, flustered by the scrutiny. Bright sun washed his hair with gold glints, playing on the damp curls formed on his brow during the afternoon heat.

"I was wondering what to wear," she mumbled.

"Whatever you choose I'm sure will be charming," he dismissed, glancing at his watch. "Though I hate to end our sightseeing, I'm afraid I really must take you back to your hotel. Do you mind?"

31

"No. My feet are killing me tramping all those endless marble corridors. I'll be glad of a rest. In fact, the idea of soaking in a tub is immensely appealing right now."

He smiled, his brown eyes softly intimate in their appraisal as his gaze lingered over the clinging pink knit bodice, traveling slowly to the curve of her hips. So intimate was the expression, Carrie blushed, knowing he pictured her luxuriating in her bath, the accuracy of his vivid imagination reflected in the warm brown eyes.

"Ah, that sounds like an admirable idea," was all he said as he took her straw purse from the white table, well aware of the inner confusion his expression caused. And, Carrie thought with growing aggravation, smugly pleased.

"Hey, you look great," Tim voiced in surprise as Carrie emerged from her room in a mint green quiana dress with draped sleeves and a tie belt.

"Thanks. Where's Ed?" she asked in surprise, finding Tim alone.

"Eating in his room. He had some sketches to make," Tim mumbled, his eyes scanning her appearance from head to toe, his open admiration apparent in his growing smile. "Great color with your hair. I don't remember seeing you in a dress before this trip, Carrie.

You look so different."

Please to win approval, yet not overjoyed by the sweating interest Tim Bryant showed, Carrie could not help feeling betrayed. Ed may have pressing work, but she was more inclined to think he was up to a little old fashioned match making with the most unlikeliest of candidates. Some girls might find Tim a wonderful catch, but she herself was tired of his colorless type, seeking a more exciting man, the kind she never met at home. A flamboyant, handsome man like Tristano to be exact.

Feeling guilty at her thoughts, Carrie turned her attention back to Tim who was regaling her with his bowling prowess. The dinner was delicious; a plate of scampi accompanied by a colorful salad comprised of every salad ingredient known to man, followed by *Zuppa Inglese* and sweet dessert wine. The pleasure of the meal was dimmed by Tim's grumbling about the lack of Thousand Island dressing for his salad, which he refused to eat, and ketchup for his shrimp, which he deigned to consume in any case, accompanied by a monologue about the backward cuisine of Venice.

Carrie allowed her mind to stray to thoughts of Tristano squiring some unknown Italian beauty to dinner, convinced he would never

33

mention ketchup or salad dressing, rather some romantic place he wished to take her . . .

"I suppose that italian Romeo swept you off your feet," Tim said, disturbing her pleasant fantasy. "It figures. All the women go for him."

"Oh, really," Carrie mumbled, finding her palms growing wet.

"Sure, but to him women are a dime a dozen. Ed tells me he descends like a hawk at the sight of some charming young newcomer rapidly polishing them off with about as much relish. You're better away from someone like that."

"Don't worry about me, Tim, I really can take care of myself."

Tim grinned, reaching for his cigarettes. "Fine. Just wanted to warn you. I've read all those gossip columns. You wouldn't believe the things they say."

"You're right, I wouldn't believe them." Carrie finished, smiling brightly at him, despite the dull thudding of her heart at his words."

"Want to dance?"

To her surprise Carrie found Tim to be a reasonable dancer, though he insisted on practicing the same steps he had obviously learned in a dancing class, despite the changing tempo of the music. Clasping her tighter, Tim exhibited his piece de resistance when the orchestra struck up a throbbing Latin beat.

"Let's go to the balcony," he suggested thickly against her ear, his breath damp against her skin when the dance ended.

"Okay, I bet there's a great view of the canal," Carrie agreed, knowing full well looking at the canal was the furthest thing from his mind. She did not want to deliberately put him down, yet Tim's increasing ardor was making her nervous.

It was dark on the balcony, the balmy spring air wrapping her in a humid blanket. Brilliant pink flowering vines growing from a blue painted tub, coiled about the stone parapet to fill the air with heady fragrance. The frangipani inspired Tim to unexpected heights of romance as he slipped his arm about her waist.

"Hey, we might do this more often when we get back."

Stiffening to feel his moist hand through her dress, Carrie wanted to tell him 'no way', but instead she smiled and made a lame excuse about a boyfriend who did not exist. Such a lovely romantic setting, alone in the dark, and she was with the wrong man. She could have wept out of frustration. Some other woman was probably on a moonlit balcony at this moment watching the bobbing, yellow lighted crafts bisecting pools of radiance on the black water. Oh, how much she envied her faceless rival that night, and though she had no actual reason to suspect it, Carrie wondered if that woman's name was Gabriella Santi.

"You can see all Venice from here," she said at last, breaking his embrace to lean over the balcony. Below the inkiness sparkled with beams of light from the hotel windows. Smooth gliding gondolas and their speedier sisters threaded flickering strings over the water in ever changing design. How wonderful to ride in a gondola with Tristano, experiencing a fabled moonlit journey down the Grand Canal like the lovers in those romantic novels she devoured in her younger years.

"Can't see why folks break their necks to come here," Tim commented, lighting a cigarette, the glowing end pinpointed the white blurr on his face. "If you ask me the whole package is vastly overrated."

"You really know how to squash someone's romantic evening," she snapped, annoyed at having his irritating presence to disturb her thoughts.

"Sorry, I didn't mean to do that. I suppose drainage and repairing buildings doesn't seem important to the Italians, they're different from us, so, well – earthy. Besides, with all the garlic they eat, they probably don't notice the bad drains."

"Drains no less! Do you really think I'll melt with tenderness after such a romantic discussion? If you and our employer are cooking up a little action including me, you can forget it. I'm not panting for romance at any cost, so you can drop the dine and dance routine. Besides, I can find my own men if I want them," she announced.

"Don't get hacked off at me, Carrie, I'm not a sophisticated man of the world like your fancy acquaintance. I say what I mean, that's all. Don't spoil things."

"I'm not the one who brought up the delightful subject of drains," she reminded tartly.

"How about a gondola ride to make up for it? Ed said –" Tim paused, realizing he had inadvertantly betrayed a confidence.

"Oh, so this was his idea! I thought as much. No thanks. It's ten o'clock and time for such a little innocent to be in bed."

Ignoring her sarcasm, he held aside the heavy velvet curtain as she thrust past him into the ballroom. "What about tomorrow? We'll be seeing the other client then, we could make it a memorable night."

"Sorry, I already have plans."

Taken back by her news, Tim blurted. "Hey, who with?"

"*Signor* Cavalli asked me to a grand ball."

Carrie swept past him with a tight smile and a hasty goodnight, not pausing in her ascent up the marble stair, though she was bursting to see his expression.

In the privacy of her room she succumbed to tears, not really knowing why she wept, so confused about the stirring feelings she had known since her arrival. Tim's romantic play annoyed her: Ed's encouragement in the set-up annoyed her. It was not that she was not ready for love; every nerve in her body was geared toward that fascinating handsome Italian whom she had known less than twenty-four hours. He interested her more, and annoyed her more, than any man she had ever met.

Thumping the pink pillowcase, damp with tears, Carrie uneasily admitted she was falling in love with him. Though he had never embraced her, never kissed her in reality, she felt as if it had happened a thousand times, so drawn to him was she. He was the dark stranger of all her dreams. It wasn't fair to have found the embodiment of her fantasies in the flesh to discover he was a worldly Italian playboy whose women were probably legion. Rich, sought after, perhaps he could not

38

resist the challenge of acquiring yet another woman to add to his conquests like other men collected books, or jewelry. Yet he had said, 'when I want something'. Pressing her face into the damp pillow, Carrie recalled his expression when he made that statement, the picture sending a thrill of pleasure through her limbs. Tomorrow she would learn if there had been anything implied by those words.

CHAPTER 3

The Cavalli's villa was a magnificent sun washed palace of buff stone surrounded by immaculately kept formal gardens of over seventy acres. From the terraces of the villa could be seen the heraldic device of the Cavalli family; an eagle clutching pillars of gold, formed from precision clipped box hedges. To the west a vast cypress hedge was trained to mirror the ancient Roman aqueducts. All this was set against the colorful grandeur of cultivated hillsides of olive groves and fruit trees. Behind the villa clipped hollyoaks and tall cypresses stood sentinel over a garden of brilliant irises of every imaginable color.

The villa itself unfolded like pages from a

guide book and it was open to the public during the high summer months. At the same time the family *palazzo* on the Grand Canal was rented to a rich American who used it as a European base. Baroque, Rococco, Renaissance styles mingled haphazardly indoors to create a world of unbelievable beauty. Painted lacquered Venetian furniture with vast crown canopied silk draped beds marked the lavish bedrooms, while the living rooms were a sea of black and painted canvas walls of colourful scenes from antiquity. This time the artist was so highly acclaimed, the villa's guide book drew attention to the brilliantly executed scenes from Roman mythology, attributing the work to pupils of the great Leonardo.

Carrie paused before one glowing canvas all rosy, voluptuous flesh, where tearful maidens with flying golden tresses were borne by virile soldiers with grim, determination marked features. Ruthless iron men . . .

"The Rape of Sabines," Tristano supplied behind her. "Quite my favorite wall."

Tim coughed in embarrassment at the near orgiastic pose of some of the reclining figures, muttering about indecency as they moved on to more acceptable expressions of art.

The appraising look Tristano flashed her, their agreement over the merit of the colorful

40

work, drew Carrie closer to him, so that they shared a secret communication.

Later, while Tim and Ed relaxed on the sun drenched terrace, hugging chilled glasses of wine, Tristano asked Carrie if she would like to see the rare white peacocks.

Agreeing she would, despite Ed's disapproving glance, Carrie ignored Tim's vague discouragement about the late hour. She almost felt the need to ask their permission, she realized in annoyance, before she accompanied her host.

Shaking off the feeling, Carrie walked swiftly beside Tristano along the long clipped cypress walk, admiring the beautiful vista stretching for miles around them glimpsed in cameo through each dark green archway as they passed. Baroque churches amid clustered red tiled roofs and sparce, pointed trees, dotted the hillside.

"Tristano."

A voice hailed them and turning they saw a man in blue slacks jogging towards them.

"My neighbor," Tristano muttered, his face darkening.

Catching his breath, the jogger slowed, his wide mouth lifting in a smile of approval as Carrie came into clear vision, slenderly attractive in an orange sleeveless dress.

"*Ciao*. Introduce me to the lovely girl."

41

"Carrie, this is Bruno – *Signorina* Neal, one of your future business associates."

Carrie smiled, not mistaking the open approval in those prominent brown eyes. "Are you the Prince from next door?"

He grinned, dashing his hand impatiently over his brow where his hair fell damply in clever concealment of a receding hairline. "Without my crown I'm very ordinary. But yes you have it. Are you the American designer?"

"His secretary."

"Too bad, I've never worked with a lady designer, it might have been fun."

"The *Signore* is on the terrace. If you hurry maybe you can catch him," Tristano suggested, his hand hovering protectively about Carrie's waist.

"Perhaps I'll jog over and make his acquaintance," Bruno suggested, though he seemed in no haste to leave as his gaze slid appreciatively to Carrie's shapely nylon stockinged legs. "I hope you intend to accompany your employer to my home. I assure you, there'll be reams of paperwork, *Signorina*," he said, his gaze moving up to her face, approval for what he saw plain in his expression.

"You'd better be sure Sophia's present, you wouldn't want to rouse her jealousy,"

Tristano warned, beginning to walk away.

"The *Principessa* will also be delighted to make your acquaintance. Well, it seems Tristano's anxious to keep you to himself, so I'll be on my way. My turn comes tomorrow. *Ciao, Bellissima.*" With this he resumed his easy pace, moving rapidly over the lawns.

Tristano watched him, his nostrils flaring in anger. "Let me warn you against Bruno, he already has a whole string of victims to his name."

"Does he get mentioned in the gossip columns too?" Carrie asked sweetly.

Snorting in disdain, Tristano turned to her. "Oh, so you believe that rubbish do you? Yes, Bruno certainly comes in for his share because there's a lot more scandal to recount about him. He already gave you that predatory look. He couldn't take his eyes from you."

"Maybe I enjoyed it."

Face darkened in anger, Tristano gripped her wrist, pulling her roughly about. "I told you to stay away from him, that's what I meant. Young women should not travel alone, it gives men the wrong impression."

"I'm not alone and because of that, as I remember, you got quite a different, if equally wrong, impression.

They glared at each other, both aware of unspoken thoughts hovering beneath the

43

surface. "Don't go off alone with him. As long as the *Principessa* is there, you've no worries."

"Oh, thank you very much for your advice. You seem to forget I am able to be my own judge."

"No you are not. It's like a lamb amongst the wolves."

"How have you got the nerve to make a statement like that after all I know about you?" she exploded, wrenching free.

Speechless he stared at her, his face stony, then seizing her fingers he propelled her rapidly along. "That's different."

"Why?"

"I know Bruno's roving eye, besides, he's married. I'm not."

Against such illogical reasoning, Carrie had no defence.

"Why don't we forget it. How about those peacocks?"

"Yes, if you're still interested," was all he said.

"I'm interested."

It was pleasing to have Tristano so obviously jealous, yet he annoyed her by his possessive behavior. Though she did not intend to encourage the Prince in his amorous intentions, having Tristano so fiercely protective of her virtue was rather flattering.

"This is such a beautiful, fairytale house, I never believed people actually lived in places like this," she breathed, when they finally entered the wrought iron gateway leading to the aviary.

"Nowadays they don't. That's why the di Monde's plan to turn theirs into a hotel. Once upon a time all the rich lived in these showplaces, each trying to outdo his rival with lavish landscaping and elaborate buildings. We have a set of private apartments on the upper floor, not half as grand. I didn't take you there because they're still being prepared for residence. Next week they'll be ready, then a long hot summer of milling visitors begins."

"Nevertheless it's still yours, even if you must share it. Have you no family?"

"My father's in Switzerland. I have a sister, Lucia, who studies art in Florence, then Guido, my younger brother, who's hiking somewhere in Greece at the moment."

Carrie smiled. "What a family of wanderers."

"Yes, aren't we. I'm the only one who was a good boy and stayed home."

"A good boy," she echoed, glancing sideways at him. "Now, is that a true description?"

His throaty chuckle echoed through the

stone walled enclosure. "Hardly, as far as your associates are concerned anyway. To them I'm a decidedly *bad* boy. Though secretly they probably envy men with reputations like mine, able to pick and choose from a vast selection of interested females. The marvelous commodity of status and wealth making that selection possible. It also encourages legions of gold diggers prompted by ambitious Mamas."

"After admitting that, you still warn me against Prince di Monde?"

Tristano grinned. "My intentions are strictly honorable, as they say. You can bet Bruno's are not."

There were two pale pink cockatoos, the only inhabitants of the small aviary. The rare white peacocks strutted lordly over the clipped grass, seeming strangely colorless.

"The birds are lovely, but they don't look like peacocks to me. I prefer the blue green variety I'm used to," Carrie admitted, leaning against a wrought iron ballustrade to view the birds, shuddering when one of them screamed with amazing human sound.

"They are kept for their rarity. Once my father had a fine bird collection, now they're gone. Since his accident he hasn't had the inclination to manage the place."

"Accident?"

"Yes, he was injured in a car wreck several

years ago. His spine is permanently damaged. He comes home for a month each year. Apart from that he stays in a private hospital in Switzerland."

"Oh, I'm so sorry, I'd no idea," she whispered in surprise, wondering if she had inadvertently opened a painful wound. Was this the secret which had been hinted in his brooding dark face? "Is your father old?"

"Not in years," Tristano paused, then turning towards her, he looked deep in her eyes, surprising her by the intensity of his expression. "I drove the car in which he was riding. There are those who have virtually accused me of being too impatient to inherit his title. Vicious nonsense, of course, but sometimes I think my father wonders . . ." he stopped abruptly and turned away, not wanting to meet her eyes.

"What cruel lies! Who'd believe something like that?"

A gentle smile curved his mouth. "Bruno, for one. You're very sweet, Carrie, don't let anyone spoil that quality. It's rare these days."

"Sweet?" Carrie echoed, not sure she enjoyed the distinction. Sweet somehow implied naive, simple, an image she did not want to keep.

"Most of the women I know are hardly

that," he said, slipping his brown hand over her own where she gripped the metal railing.

The warmth of his touch accelerated her emotion, until Carrie found absurd grief stinging her eyes. He seemed sad; how much she wanted to bring a smile to his face. "Maybe you know the wrong women," she said.

"Rich young bachelors always attract the 'wrong sort', as you put it. Money hungry women of the world, all grabbing frantically at security."

"Surely money isn't their only interest?" With surprise Carrie heard herself voice that thought, found his hand moving along her arm as he traced the down of blond hair.

"No, you are right, I do have a certain reputation to uphold. My ancestors were renowned lovers of women. They tell me I've inherited that trait."

Boldly their eyes met, Carrie wanted to look away, yet she could not. When he moved towards her, when his arm slipped warmly about her shoulders, she knew he would kiss her. She wanted the kiss, actively seeking his mouth with her own. When their lips touched the longed for kiss made time stand still. Carrie found her knees going weak. Sensing her faltering stance, Tristano tightened his arms to hold her upright when their lips parted.

"Ah, *Carissima*, how I wish you were spending the summer here. You are so different from other women, so freshly alive . . ."

A pointed throat clearing turned their attention to the path where Ed, and a scarlet faced Tim Bryant, stood selfconsciously watching. Leaning casually against the railing was the Prince di Monde, clearly enjoying the romantic interlude, obviously feeling it increased his own chances of success tomorrow. Tristano released her, showing no embarrassment at being caught in such a condemning position; in contrast, Carrie flushed brick red, finding no words to excuse this public lapse from sanity.

Throughout the afternoon there was a strained undercurrent at the villa. Even on the return journey, speeding along the *autostrada* in Tristano's yellow car squashed like sardines on the plush upholstery, Carrie hunched miserably against the door, sticky with perspiration. A beautiful experience was turned tawdry by discovery, making her feel cheap, robbing the embrace of some of its magic. The others thought her bowled over by Tristano's experienced line while he took advantage of her innocence; it's not like that, she wanted to shout, I'm not another easy conquest.

The splendid *Palazzos* along the canal radiated shimmering yellow pools across the water, the sound of laughter and throbbing music audible long before the slow moving gondola reached the Santi landing stage. Moored boats creaked in the swelling water as they passed. The silver crescent moon hid behind shifting clouds robbing the spring evening of moonlight to heighten the romance of this journey. Even Tristano, resplendent in period costume of rose velvet sparkled with gold, was unusually withdrawn.

Stealing a nervous glance at his dark, brooding face, Carrie wondered if he too regretted the interruption of their privacy this afternoon. Perhaps, for her own safety, her colleagues' appearance was fortunate. A few moments more of the insane beauty of Tristano's touch and heaven alone knows where it would have ended, Carrie thought, chewing the cherry frost lipstick from her lower lip as she nervously reviewed her own vulnerability. Was he trying to warn her against romantic involvement when he mentioned the kind of woman he usually dated? Yet what about his 'honorable intentions' as opposed to Bruno's of a

50

decidedly different nature? It was so confusing. Those sophisticated socialites Tristano usually dated were not the kind to wave fond farewells when the clock struck midnight. If she was to continue any sort of relationship with him, she must first decide if she was prepared to give her heart to a man like that.

"It looks like fog, eh, Roberto?"

"Si, *Signore*, rolling in from the sea. Look, you can't see the Basilica. Even the bridge wears a halo."

They spoke in English for her benefit. Carrie looked where the gondolier pointed: ahead loomed the famed Rialto Bridge, that venerable antiquity lined with shops and spanning the narrowest part of the Grand Canal. The stone bridge was wreathed in streamers of white. The mist billowed like trailing ghosts between the ornate spans, softening the stone parapet with clouds of shifting vapor. The fog shadowed everything to form a sad, almost forbidding scene so that she unconsciously drew closer to Tristano for protection, shivering in the damp night air.

"Are you cold, *Cara?*" he asked solicitously, eyeing the thin pale dress with its openwork crocheted lace. "Such a lovely gown wasn't meant for gondola rides in the fog."

"It's all right. I have a shawl." She wrapped

the lacy knitted fabric about her shoulders, finding it added little warmth.

Lazily smiling at her for the first time since he met her at the hotel landing stage, Tristano slid his arm about her shoulders, drawing her close against the heat of his body. "Come, we'll warm each other."

And though his words sent a thrill of warmth tingling through her limbs, Carrie could not dispel the melancholy created by the fog shrouded canal. Somewhere in one of those bright *palazzos* waited Gabriella Santi. In a few minutes she would meet the woman who flitted disembodied through her thoughts, as much a wraith as the fogbanks. She would learn if Gabriella was more than a friend to Tristano.

The bobbing striped poles, the battery of wrought iron lanterns marking the *Palazzo Santi*, loomed ahead in a blaze of light. Roberto had burst into song on the final stretch of their journey, his pleasant baritone muffled by the pillows of white through which they glided, invisible one moment, then coming out on the light splashed ripples as the billowing clouds skipped upstream. The lilting love song turned the gondola ride into a romantic escapade. Pointedly he averted his gaze, not looking back at his passengers, concentrating instead on the fog wisped waterway.

"Roberto's being very gallant. He probably thinks I'm making love to you," Tristano whispered, his breath warmly fanning her face.

Carrie smiled but secretly she knew disappointment. If that was the usual turn of events when Tristano Cavalli took a woman for a gondola ride, why had he not even tried to kiss her?

Then there was little time to supply an answer to her question for they were stepping on the chill, water rocked platform, Tristano's warm hands safely steadying her passage. Surrounded by the ancient *palazzos* with their weathered facades, the bobbing high prowed craft lit garishly by black filigree lanterns, Carrie experienced the strange sensation of being thrust back five hundred years. Tristano in his bright velvet garments, his soft kidskin boots and glittering tights, could have been the powerful nobleman who built *Palazzo* Cavalli. The possessive way in which he slipped his arm warmly about her waist, after thanking the boatman, only adding to the illusion.

Carrie blinked to clear her vision, loathe to dismiss that pleasant dream as they went upstairs, music throbbing the ancient *palazzos* walls as they walked through gloom until the vast main room exploded before them in light and warmth like a priceless pearl set in the heart of the dark rambling building. Silks, satins, glowed beneath the blazing crystal chandeliers, each light fixture a masterpiece in itself. Colored glass flowers of remarkable execution shone among the scintillating glass, dazzling her eyes. Costumes of various periods promoted that feeling of being thrust into antiquity. Assorted accompaniments of definitely twentieth century parties finally dispelled the illusion. Hors d'oeuvres and glasses of champagne on vast silver trays covered trestle tables at the end of the room. This sudden intrusion was disillusioning. How lovely to have been able to drift forever in that limbo of the past with Tristano at her side.

"*Caro*, how lovely to have you here."

The soft modulated voice stiffened Carrie's spine. Even before she turned to meet the owner of that honeyed tone she knew that would be Gabriella.

"Gaby, you look exquisite. Renaissance costume was designed just for you," Tristano complimented, seizing her hand and planting a soft kiss on the palm.

Raising her eyes from his bent dark head, Gabriella Santi viewed Carrie with a coldly assessing stare. "And who's this little girl?"

54

she drawled when Tristano straightened up.

He grinned, pulling a wry face when he saw tension mount in Carrie's face. "Not a little girl, Sweetest, but a very lovely young woman from the firm of Stern and Associates. Here for business."

Gabriella smiled stiffly, and Carrie saw the telltale flash of jealousy in the woman's long green eyes. The revelation pleased her, yet the change in Tristano's behavior as he wandered from group to group sharing jokes and laughter as he renewed old acquaintanceships, robbed her of pleasure. It was as if he had forgotten her existence.

Able to study Gabriella at a distance without being observed, Carrie became freshly jealous of her. Her perfect oval face was translucent ivory with long green eyes glinting yellow like a cat's above those high slanted cheekbones. When she smiled with her rose red mouth, so perfect it appeared to have been drawn on canvas by a master's brush, she revealed even white teeth, which though probably capped, were not diminished in their flashing beauty. Gabriella's honey colored hair was trapped inside a jeweled net dotted with rubies to match her red satin gown trimmed with gold embroidered roses. When she stood in the shadows at the head of the curving marble stair Gabriella looked like a figure from an old master miraculously brought to life. To think she had secretly hoped to outdazzle the mysterious Gabriella in Tristano's eyes!

"Say, are you American?"

Carrie turned to find a middle-aged woman attired in a white Grecian gown trimmed in a scroll design of gold braid. Her immaculate bouffant hair style washed with a blue rinse seemed out of place against the classic simplicity of the floating silk dress.

"Yes."

"Oh, great, I was beginning to feel lost with all these foreigners. Here on vacation?" The woman asked, slipping a friendly ringed hand under Carrie's elbow, shepherding her towards an empty couch beneath the curtained window.

"Just a couple of days on business," Carrie replied absently, as she searched the crowd for Tristano's striking rose velvet costume. While some of the other men looked strange in doublet and cloak, Tristano moved with such ease he might have worn this elaborate attire every day. The natural swagger to his step sent the short, gold trimmed cape swinging jauntily from his wide shoulders, adding emphasis to their width in startling contrast to the narrowness of his hips. Carrie spotted him at last, offering a glass of champagne to a tall figure in dark red velvet and her

56

heart lurched sickeningly as Gabriella tilted her head to gaze longingly in his dark eyes. As Carrie watched his hand steal to that graceful ivory neck, gently fondling before moving to the elaborate coiled hair arrangement, the intimacy of the gesture nauseated her. Her jealousy was aroused by the scene. As she forced her gaze from the striking couple she found to her distress, her companion had been talking to her all this time. Guiltily she began to apologize until she discovered the woman had not even noticed her inattention, so wrapped up was she in her own speech.

"A fantastic party, isn't it? Like something right out of Hollywood. They tell me some big movie stars are stopping by later. We might just get our pictures in the paper. How do you fancy making it to one of the gossip columns?"

"I don't think I'm interesting enough for that," Carrie mumbled, lifting the heavy gold fringed curtain to look down on the canal. The fog had closed in more densely so that the lanterns made orange blurs through the swirling white. The desolate scene chilled her and she dropped the curtain back in place, feeling very much alone.

"Can I bring you something to drink, *Cara?*"

The unexpected voice at her elbow sent her

nerves tingling. Tristano leaned towards her, fighting against the surge of guests, standing his ground.

"Yes, I'll take champagne."

"Stay right here. I'll bring it to you."

Carrie drew herself up stiffly, squaring her shoulders, holding her head high. Finally he had noticed her; she had half expected to be marooned with this chatty tourist for the duration of the party. Still, she must not be too harsh in her judgement of him. People had crowded round embracing him as the Italians were wont to do, asking about his latest exploits she was sure by the knowing grins, the laughter, at his swift replies. It had all taken place in Italian so she could not translate their conversation, but her own vivid imagination easily supplied the topic.

"He's that Conte all the women are wild about, isn't he?" the woman beside her gushed breathlessly, following his broad shouldered figure towards the refreshment table with pop-eyed gaze.

"Tristano Cavalli? He's not a conte," Carrie corrected.

"Not yet, but he soon will be. I read something about him just the other day. And all the different women he's seen with. Wow, he really has something going for him. Looks and money are what counts. And, honey, he

58

has the lot. How did *you* meet him? You don't strike me as the type."

"We're business associates."

"Oh, is that all." Disinterest turned the nasal voice to a whine and the other woman looked away. "Say, never did ask your name, or where you're from. Mine's Myrtle Tannenbaum – you know, like the Christmas carol – from St. Louis."

"I'm Caroline Neal, from Oklahoma." Carrie used her full name to make it sound more sophisticated, though hers won hands down over something as bizarre as Myrtle Tannenbaum.

"Do you know her too? The Princess."

"Princess?" Carrie repeated in surprise, thinking perhaps the Princess di Monde was also a guest. When she followed Myrtle's voracious gaze, as she virtually gobbled up the glamorous celebrities, Carrie discovered she watched no other but Gabriella Santi who stood at the door of the vast salon to welcome a party of late arrivals. "You mean Gabriella?"

"Surely you knew she was a princess? They probably don't use the title for anything but show these days. She's a real blue blood. On first name basis, huh? How about introducing me? I don't know anyone else here beside Hank." She pointed towards a fat man in evening dress who puffed desperately on a

59

large cigar. "My brother-in-law. He wangled this invite. I wouldn't miss it for the world. Introduce me, honey, that'd be something to tell the folks back home. Fancy, meeting a real princess. She's the one who's going to marry that conte. Got that from a gossip column in the London papers. 'Inside source reveals nuptuals' – you know the crap, anyway, two better suited people you couldn't find. I bet her kids'll win beauty contests hands down."

Stiffly in shock, Carrie sat as if frozen to the hard seat, waving mutely to Myrtle as she clumped away for a little more action. Tristano and Gabriella to be married! Though everything in those gossip columns could not be believed, she was a firm believer in the old adage 'where there's smoke there's fire'. That gesture, those intimate smiles she had intercepted, only added credibility to the story. Of all the nerve, telling her to stay away from the Prince, when he was engaged to another woman! Some honorable intentions! Carrie wanted to scream in her rage as she watched him moving towards her, oblivious to her secret knowledge.

"Here, sorry I took so long. It's like a battle now they're dancing," he said, thrusting the chilled champagne in her cold hand. "Your hands are like ice. Are you still cold?"

"No, I'm fine, thanks," she dismissed

60

stiffly. For some absurd reason when she saw him smiling down at her, she wanted to cry instead of lash out at him in rage. He had been so attentive, so romantic with his burning, dark-eyed gaze, his caresses which she had thought special for her. His attraction had helped her overlook his possessive streak, the undercurrent of disapproval for her working so far from home; if the truth were out, probably for her working *period*. In true Italian macho style he probably expected his women to stay home ready to dance attendance on him when he deigned to show up, almost like a harem. There he stood, supremely arrogant in his masculinity, glancing critically over the pretty girls. To think all this time she had hoped he was falling in love with her, he was virtually engaged to the glamorous Princess Gabriella!

"Finished?" he asked in surprise, as the last of the champagne rapidly disappeared. "Come, will you dance with me? I want to show you off."

Pain formed a giant lump in her throat. When he took her arm, his hand hot through the thin cotton sleeve, Carrie found her limbs grown heavy, tingling; whether the reaction came from the champagne, or Tristano's nearness, she did not know.

His arms about her, the vast magnetic aura

he produced gripping her with intoxicating force, Carrie swept about the dance floor into the adjoining room. At last he held her in his arms, he made soft, intimate conversation as he fixed her with that brooding, unfathomable gaze. She had waited an eternity for this and when it came it was all pointless because he belonged to Gabriella. She could never hope to compete with that rich, beautiful princess. Whether it was only a courtesy title or not, the blood of princess still flowed in her veins, those centuries of breeding reflected in the lovely Gabriella's every move. She would be as at home in the luxurious villa with its antiques, as she was here in Palazzo Santi with the painted cream satin panels on the walls, the rooms glittering with vast crystal chandeliers sparkling like so many diamonds. This was where Tristano belonged. For a girl from small town U.S.A. to expect to become part of that glittering life of luxury was laughable.

When he released her, taking her back to her seat, Carrie found her eyes stinging with tears. She did not cling to his warm hand which slid affectionately into her own much as she longed to do; she did not even catch his rose velvet sleeve to detain him when Gabriella called his name. The romance she had headily indulged in these past magic hours in Venice had been solely a figment of her own imagination. And she could have sunk through the floor in humiliation for her own foolish expectations.

About her swirled throbbing music, lights and noise, until Carrie found her head bursting. Fighting her way across the bright room, she slipped into the cool dark corridor outside, thankful to be able to hide her embarrassment in private. In a couple of days she would fly home. Once she would never have thought she would feel this way, but now she could hardly wait to feel that upsurge as the jet became airborne. Once aboard she knew she would never set eyes on the disturbing figure of Tristano Cavalli again.

Leaning her face against the cool comfort of the gilded woodwork in the corridor, Carrie admitted she did not really want that, though once home she would be safely distant from his attraction, she would also be terribly alone. All the men she knew would never match Tristano in her dreams. What irony to have found that image come to life at last, only to learn he was unattainable. Tristano would have needed little encouragement to have a brief, passionate affair with her, in fact, he seemed to have been inviting it this afternoon in the secluded beauty of the aviary garden. That type of hasty encounter was not what she craved. How stupid of her to project her own standards on a man like Tristano. He unabashedly liked women, he loved them and just as predictably left them; there was no more to it than that. To expect a lasting commitment from him was ridiculous. Even Gabriella, who was virtually his bride, could not expect that. The suspicion, the jealous flash betrayed in her eyes, told Carrie as much. Tristano Cavalli would be difficult to hold for even a little time; his faithfulness for a lifetime was too much for any woman to expect.

A movement on the stairs alerted her and Carrie stepped back in the shadows. To her misery she saw two blurred figures close locked in an embrace; rose and wine velvet mingled in brilliant contrast to the vast marble bannister.

"Caro, how long I've waited for you. Why didn't you tell me . . ."

The words lapsed into Italian and Carrie could no longer understand. Laughing, Tristano replied in that familiar, husky voice of reassurance, the way he had done to her, stifling Gabriella's protests with a kiss. Carrie leaned against the wall and she wanted to die. It was bad enough to be haunted by doubts, but to have them demonstrate the truth of their relationship before her was too much.

Clutching her shawl tightly about her shoulders, stumbling on unsteady feet, Carrie hastened down the corridor towards the back of the house. She had no means of water transport so she must leave by the back entrance into the alleyway. At least Tristano's tour of his *palazzo* had revealed that alternate entrance to Venetian houses.

The door stuck and she wrenched it open with unusual strength. White mist swirled inside like smoke. Gasping, she wrapped the cobweb shawl about her head, and pulling it tight, she charged into the clammy night.

The mist was not dense in the alley so she managed to negotiate the journey to the first bisecting street with ease. Here the lamps shone murkily orange through the swathing blanket. Afraid of taking the wrong turning, by the smell of refuse and oil, the hollow clanking moorings, Carrie knew she had luckily turned towards the canal. She must cross the Rialto to get to her hotel.

Footsteps echoed behind her, then a man's voice shouted something through the fog. In terror she began to run, not knowing where she went, only curving towards the sound of the Grand Canal. Who pursued her? She had heard stories of assassins lurking through the byways of Italian cities, of roaming vagabonds bent on assaulting young, unaccompanied women. Faster, faster, she ran until with relief she saw the unmistakable shape of the Rialto between the buildings.

Stumbling, she wrenched her ankle, but it was not severe enough to halt her flight. The shuttered shops seemed sinister in the fog as if countless unknown figures lurked in the doorways awaiting her passage. Vast billows, gray white swirled over the bridge, momentarily halting her steps. So dense was the fog Carrie could not make out the other end of the bridge. She stopped, her heart beating a deafening tattoo as the sound of pursuit grew clearer through the blanketing white. A breeze suddenly lifted the cloud so that it wisped upward like a wraith toward the rooves of the shuttered shops, up, up, till it floated over the canal, leaving trailing streamers of vapor. At least now she could see the beckoning just yards away where her hotel waited in all its friendliness, where Ed and Tim ate dinner in the gilded dining room.

"You little fool!"

Spinning about, Carrie cried out in shock as the thud of steps terminated in the floating shreds of gray. Arms reached for her. Her scream was muffled by a man's hand and when she was jerked about to face her assailant she saw the rose pink velvet doublet of a bygone era. She knew it was Tristano as

66

she tried to still her thudding fright, but the sudden appearance from the swirling mist of this figure in Renaissance garb here on the ancient Rialto was a terrifying sight.

"I'm real. No ghost. Pull yourself together," he hissed, his dark face grim in the blurred yellow lights. "Don't scream," he cautioned, removing his hand.

"You! Why didn't you identify yourself," she demanded in anger and fright, suddenly aware of shaking legs.

"You wouldn't stop. I've been shouting to you since I saw you run into the alley. It was a stupid thing to do, charging out in the fog. Being out alone is bad enough at night. Do you want to end up in the canal?" he growled, tightening his grip in anger.

"What would you care if I did?" she challenged, trying to push him away, but not able to move his looming bulk.

"Why do you say a thing like that?"

"Because you only wanted another conquest. I thought – oh damn you, for what I thought. It's not really your fault." She was crying now, vast streams of grief running through the carefully applied beige makeup, bringing tracers of black from her mascaraed eyes. "Why didn't you tell me about Gabriella? At least you – you could've told me – instead of – then having the nerve to tell me to stay away from Bruno, as if you owned me – oh, let me go. Leave me some self respect."

Anger flashed through his face. "Tell you *what* about me and Gabriella? She's no more to me than a dozen others have been."

Carrie gasped, struggling, trying to wrench free. To her surprise he suddenly let her go so that she fell sideways against the painted door of a nearby shop.

"There. I won't hold you against your will. Go, you stupid, frightened little girl. What did you expect from me? We kissed. What did I promise with a kiss?"

In misery Carrie pulled her shawl protectively around her shoulders, mustering all her dignity, which was not easy with a throbbing ankle and striped, tear-stained face.

"Nothing," she managed, forcing her voice not to tremble. "It was just, when you got so angry about the Prince, when you – oh, nothing, but my own assumption you meant something. Now, will you let me go back to my hotel, or must I fight you off?"

"Tristano Cavalli never has to fight for a woman. There are too many eager ones for that," he announced, drawing himself to his full height, giving an arrogant toss of his head. "Go to your hotel. Run away to your friends and spill the whole terrible story

68

of your shocking treatment," he snarled in scorn. "And tomorrow, when Bruno turns on all his devious charm, I won't breathe a word of protest. He is all yours – the answer to a maiden's prayer," he mocked, his lips curled in a sneer.

Anger, pain, humiliation, seized Carrie and she stepped forward, her hand raised to strike his handsome, arrogant face, to wipe away that smug assurance. Like lightning he gripped her wrist bending her swiftly towards him. Tristano kissed her deeply, his mouth devouring hers, so that against her will she relaxed her guard for the few moments it took with his mouth pressed over hers.

With a scornful laugh, he stepped back. "There, *Signorina*, that will be something for you to remember during those long months ahead. Too bad your narrow ideas of moral virtue got in the way. I never lied to you. Everything I said was the truth, whether you believe it or not."

Then he was gone, striding back across the bridge, his pink garments receding in the fog. Frozen, Carrie waited till the sound of his steps died away, then she sprang to action, racing the rest of the way over the bridge, running toward her hotel down the narrow alley, tripping over garbage and marauding cats in her mad flight to safety. The mocking picture of his face tormented her as she ran, seeming to dance before her, handsome and masterful like a disembodied wraith in the floating streamers of white fog.

CHAPTER 4

Tears stung Carrie's eyes as she fumbled blindly for the revolving door at the hotel entrance. Like a drowning soul she grasped the cold metal and pushed her way inside the hotel lobby. At this late hour everywhere was deserted. Carrie was thankful for small favors; now no one would see how disheveled she looked. One glance in the mirrored wall told her that the party look she had gone to such pains to create to impress Tristano, was a disaster. She shuddered at the unwelcome reminder of his existence. Everytime she thought about their heated quarrel on the bridge she wanted to burst into tears of humiliation.

Only when Carrie was able to close her bedroom door on the world, did she feel comforted. It took great self-control not to succumb to her first inclination to throw herself on the bed and have a good cry;

instead she switched on the light and studied her ravaged appearance in the dressing table mirror. She looked like a circus clown with her panda ringed eyes and straggling hair. What an end to a perfect evening!

Oh, Tristano Cavalli, how I hate you, she muttered to the empty room. Though obviously he could not hear her condemnation, the very speaking of the hostile words soothed her feelings. He was a cheap Italian romeo, a playboy, a wolf! All the epithets she had ever heard to describe his type sprang to her lips. At least he had taught her a lesson: when an Italian man paid her flowery compliments which she found hard to believe, she had better listen to her commonsense. Compliments like that were nothing but a pack of lies spoken merely to seduce her into his own way of thinking. The worse part of all was that she had fallen for Tristano's practised line like a schoolgirl.

Pausing at the windows in her angry march about the room, Carrie deliberately turned her back on the fog wreathed canal, for the sight awakened too many painful memories. And though she was well-armed against Tristano's charms in the immediate future, the loss of her beautiful dream world still caused her pain. Now, when she looked in the mirror, Carrie Neal seemed plainer than ever: Gabriella's

71

image seemed to be reflected behind her, her glamorous, almost feline beauty a mocking contrast. To think she had been conceited enough to imagine she could compete with a woman like Gabriella Santi!

Later, when Carrie lay sleepless on the luxurious bed, she realized her confidence had come from the assumption that Tristano felt affection for her. She shivered in the damp air drifting through the windows, full of the smells of the canal, and she blinked back tears as she thought how handsome he was, so totally unlike any other man she had ever known, or could ever hope to know in her hometown, that she had fallen head over heels in love with him. Regardless of Gabriella Santi's existence, Carrie had to admit she loved him. Though the idea of sharing him with another did not appeal to her. In the damp blackness, with the serenade of hooting foghorns in the background, Carrie allowed her painful tears to fall.

It was nearly dawn when she fell asleep to dream of being pursued by a masked figure whose identity was hidden in the swirling mist.

A discreet knock on the bedroom door roused her from the first sound sleep she had enjoyed all night. Sleepily, Carrie rubbed her eyes and she peered at the clock: it was already eight o'clock.

"Carrie, are you ready? It's time for breakfast."

It was Tim. Too bad he couldn't have been the one being pursued by Gabriella, she thought in a weak attempt at humor; but then, even fantasy only went so far!

"Okay, Tim. Give me a few minutes. I overslept."

"I'll be back in ten minutes."

"Fine."

Reluctantly Carrie slid from under the warm bedcovers. The marble floor was icy to her feet and she quickly scuffled about under the bed in search of her slippers. The vast room was washed with light as it filtered through the curtains, that lovely, special Venetian light which reminded her painfully of yesterday.

While she washed and dressed Carrie almost succeeded in convincing herself she was acting like an idiot over the man. Yet however hard she tried to be cheerful, she could not squelch the pain aroused by the discovery of the love affair between Gabriella and Tristano. Besides, after her quarrel with him last night, even if there had not been another woman in the background, she doubted if he would give her the time of day. He was a typical Latin male who needed to dominate a woman. The

73

mere thought of one speaking up to him, or daring to challenge his ideas, was enough to send him racing away to easier conquests.

Easier! Carrie laughed scornfully at her pale reflection in the mirror. Who could have been any easier? She had practically fallen in his arms, so bowled over by his charms had she been. That romantic kiss in the garden, all his compliments, had been a part of a calculated plan of campaign, in just the very manner in which he accused the Prince di Monde of mapping a route of conquest. Carrie paused, her lipstick in mid-air. She had forgotten the Prince di Monde with his warmly appraising eyes and his flattering compliments. She had also forgotten how livid Tristano had been at the thought of her even speaking to the Prince, let alone taking him up on any suggestions to further their acquaintance. How would Tristano feel if he saw her dancing with the Prince?

The idea brought a fresh sparkle to Carrie's eyes. She had just discovered a cure for her blues. Though she may never have Tristano, she was certainly not going to let him think she was hanging around moping about it. Two could play a flirtatious game. What harm would it do? After all, she would be far away before the aging playboy could press his suit. In exchange for those few minutes of triumph when she had watched the anger flaring in Tristano's face at the thought of her attentions being given to another man, the price of suffering the Prince's attentions was a small one to pay. After all, he was a prince, and not an unattractive one at that, despite their age difference. Bruno di Monde may not be the man of her dreams, but in order to arouse that man, he would be an admirable substitute.

Carrie critically surveyed her appearance in the mirror finding her face appeared too pale against her navy striped suit. Giving her cheeks an extra dab of blusher to add the illusion of health and vitality, she walked to the door.

The hotel was just the same as it had been yesterday morning, Carrie reminded herself as she went to the dining room, yet what had then seemed exquisite had somehow faded to disclose a shabby attempt at luxury on the management's behalf. Her disillusion with Tristano extended to include the somewhat threadbare carpeting, the tarnished gilt fringe on the faded velvet curtains, the unsightly chipped paint: even the too shiny seat of the *Maitre d's* suit came in for its share of criticism.

"You sure are quiet today," Tim commented as he sipped his coffee. "Anything wrong?"

75

"No. I guess I didn't sleep too well."

"Who would with those darned horns blaring away. It was almost midnight before I got to sleep myself."

Nearly midnight! A small stab of pain twisted in Carrie's heart at the phrase. Like Cinderella, her visions of a handsome prince had melted away at the stroke of midnight when she raced through the fog wreathed streets; but unlike the fairytale heroine, she had not left behind her glass slipper for her prince to find. Their heated exchange had destroyed all remnants of delight. Tristano had been brutal with her! His mouth had bruised hers in that demanding kiss. Yet the memory of the touch of his mouth against her own had the ability to begin that heady merry-go-round of dreams all over again.

They left the dining room and joined Ed Stern in the lobby. Carrie found the need to act as if nothing had happened was becoming a decided strain. It was hard to smile with delight at her surroundings as she had done so easily yesterday when the exciting panorama of Venice had spread before her like a dream come true. Today disillusion had made her bitter.

On the river taxi a young Italian treated Carrie to an admiring glance, his large brown eyes as soulful as a puppy's. Yesterday she

76

would have blushed with delight at his interest: today his unspoken invitation left her cold. There were too many reminders of Tristano in his hot-eyed interest for comfort. So Carrie deliberately turned her back on him to stare with unseeing eyes across the wide expanse of sparkling water.

When they passed the Cavalli Palazzo, Carrie became conscious of her heart fluttering in a sickening wave of panic, for she saw a man waving to them from the balcony. Surely he could not be Tristano! Then, as she saw the black shape of a pair of binoculars held up to his eyes, she knew her most sickening suspicions were confirmed. It was Tristano. And he was looking straight at her. Carrie could feel his eyes boring into her and the discomfort of his scrutiny brought blood flooding to her cheeks until her face burned. How humiliating to know he was watching her reactions, yet not be able to face him eye to eye. Watching her through binoculars was like spying.

"Hey, aren't you going to wave?" Ed asked in surprise. "That's Tristano up there on the balcony."

Carrie stiffly raised her hand, but her fingers seemed to be glued together so that her response was like a wooden marionette's.

The Prince di Monde had sent a chauffeur

77

driven car to take them to his estate. As they sped along the *autostrada* in air conditioned luxury, Carrie found she had far too much time to brood. Even the picture postcard scenes whipping past the windows were a reminder of yesterday. At least she was not expected to join the conversation, for the Prince's driver, who had a brother in Chicago, plied Ed with a million questions, the answering of which occupied them until they were in sight of the villa.

"I guess Tristano's coming out later," Ed said as they passed the Cavalli villa. "He said he had some business to attend to this morning. At least this way we can get right down to it with the Prince di Monde."

Tim agreed with Ed that it was for the best while he inwardly cheered at the thought that Tristano would be absent at least for the morning. He had been too conscious of the Italian's presence yesterday, and even more conscious of his ulterior motives where Carrie was concerned. And though she hotly denied being unable to take care of herself, Tim knew a girl like Carrie was completely out of her depth where an international jet-setter like Romeo Cavalli was concerned.

"Say this is real nice, huh, Carrie?"

Carrie nodded her agreement as they stepped from the limousine onto a gravel

78

driveway bordered with yellow and purple iris. The Di Monde's stucco villa gleamed sparkling white in the bright sunshine. At first glance it was not unlike the Cavalli villa, with the exception of two broad loggias extending on either side of the main building. Vast curtains of flowering vines draped the masonry adding soft smudges of pink, mauve and blue to the austere masonry. It was a beautiful home set like a jewel in an intricately landscaped park which stretched toward a lake shimmering in the distance. Ed had been right when he had suggested this home as the perfect setting for an exclusive hotel.

They were ushered inside the cool interior of the villa. Carrie was struck by the vastness of the hallway which seemed large enough to be a ballroom. Here, as at the Cavalli properties, pieces of sculpture were displayed in lighted niches around the walls of the circular room. In the center of the entrance hall was a triple basin fountain which splashed a musical accompaniment to their conversation.

"Wow," was the combined comment of the two men as they looked about the luxurious appointments of this villa.

Carrie too was impressed by the museum-like setting. This entire room seemed to be made of marble: the floor was black and white diamond patterned marble, while the walls had mingled gray and terra cotta veins extending to a pure white ceiling where the marble was fluted like pleated fabric inside the dome.

It was the Prince and the *Principessa* themselves who came forward to greet their guest. Carrie was surprised by the *Principessa's* appearance, for she had expected to see a slender, fashionable woman in her early forties. To her amazement she found that Sophia di Monde looked more like the Prince's mother than his wife. Her iron gray hair was scraped back in a bun, the severe style only calling attention to her angular features. The *Principessa's* skin was heavily lined, though an attempt at camouflage with an expert makeup job minimized the wrinkles, there was no way to conceal them.

Quickly swallowing her surprise, Carrie stepped forward to grasp the slender lined hand which was extended towards her.

"Welcome, *Signorina*. Come this way, if you please," said the *Principessa* in halting English.

While Carrie followed the *Principessa's* tall, thin figure through a green velvet draped archway, she became conscious of the Prince's wandering attention. Though Ed and Tim were already outlining their plans to him, his gaze was concentrated on Carrie as she walked from the room. She smiled at the reminder of his wandering eye. If this was an example the Prince di Monde would fit in splendidly with her scheme to arouse Tristano's jealousy. Oh that superior male would be in for a surprise all right. When she appeared to succumb to Bruno's very obvious attentions, Tristano would be livid. The idea turned her down mood into one of cheer as she hurried her steps to keep up with the *Principessa's* long, graceful stride.

In a beautifully appointed room where the walls were covered in rose silk brocade, Carrie was served tea from a delicate ivory rose china tea set. The dainty cup stood on small, flower-shaped feet and Carrie had to be extremely careful not to tip it over as she perched nervously on the edge of a yellow satin chair and tried to appear at home in the *Principessa* di Monde's grand salon.

"You like Venice, *Signorina?*"

"Oh, very much. What little I've seen of it, that is."

The *Principessa* smiled. "I understood Tristano took you on a guided tour."

"Well he did, but we only had time to cover the high spots," Carrie mumbled as she thankfully buried her face in her tea cup to hide the flush which she knew was spreading

81

to her hairline. The *Principessa's* knowledge was unsettling. How much more did she know about her dealings with Tristano? Or, knowing his reputation for being a lady's man, did the *Principessa* naturally assume the rest?

"He's such a handsome boy, is he not?"

"Yes, very," Carrie gulped, while she desperately wondered how she might change the subject.

"You have also met Gabriella?"

"Yes."

"I am fond of her. She is my god-daughter."

"Oh, how nice."

At that moment the men sauntered inside the room to spare Carrie from any further uncomfortable conversation. She was glad of the breather which gave her time to get her mind sorted out. She would just have to face it; these people were going to keep right on talking about Tristano whether she wanted to discuss him or not, so she must come to grips with her own feelings about him, however painful they may be. And it was painful, she must admit, as she retraced the heartbreaking picture of Tristano kissing Gabriella, then his anger when he eventually caught her after the frightening pursuit through the darkened streets of Venice. But that was life, wasn't it. Win a few, lose a few, as the saying went. She was here in Venice enjoying the hospitality of a Prince and Princess. Those memories would always be hers to treasure; this vacation would be hers when she was back home to relive at leisure. She did not need a commitment from Tristano Cavalli as well.

Though she was afraid those brave statements were far from the truth, Carrie felt better after her stern talk with her inner self. Her new resolve carried her through the next three hours while she took shorthand notes for Ed while they walked about the palatial rooms of the villa. This morning Tim revealed his working personality, which Carrie found at odds with the paunchy, homely, provincial Tim she knew and disliked. These two separate personalities were housed in a singularly unappealing body, which this morning was swathed in an ill fitting gray suit with a drab blue shirt for contrast.

When the villa had been completely covered, the party moved outside to the terrace through tall French windows. From here there was a beautiful view of the surrounding countryside and Carrie paused a moment to take it in. The men were already strolling down the wide shallow steps and she had just decided she had better run after them, when a husky voice said:

"Buon giorno, Signorina."

Carrie gasped and her hands grew clammy as she recognized Tristano's voice. What was he doing here? Hadn't he said he had bank business to complete before leaving Venice?

"Ah, she's quite lovely, your young American friend."

The *Principessa's* laughing voice joined his. Carrie knew she must turn around to acknowledge them. Very slowly she made the effort, steeling herself for the unexpected sight of him. Nothing must be betrayed before the *Principessa's* keen eyes, for she thought them still the best of friends.

"Hello. I thought you weren't coming out until this afternoon."

"I finished my business early."

Carrie gulped as she raised her eyes to meet his. So practised at deceiving, was he, she could find no trace of anger betrayed in his dark eyes. It was as if they had never quarreled last night, almost as if they were picking up where they left off after that romantic interlude in the garden.

Tristano was dressed for riding and as Carrie scanned his well fitting clothes, tailored to perfection, she forced her gaze away. The russet jacket molded and accentuated his wide shoulders, while the fawn britches seemed so sleekly fitting, she was uncomfortably aware of the rippling muscles in his thighs.

"We are going for our daily ride. Do you ride, *Signorina?*" asked the *Principessa*. When she stepped out into the sunlight she too was dressed in superbly tailored riding clothes. The entire outfit was black, except for a white scarf tucked inside the neck of her black hacking jacket.

"A little, but nothing formal," Carrie mumbled, hoping Tristano was not going to suggest she join them.

"A pity. Perhaps you will join us someday soon," he drawled as he ushered his companion to the terrace steps.

"Yes, perhaps." Carrie glanced over her shoulder to see the men already crossing the lawn towards a belt of shrubbery. "I really have to go now," she excused. "My boss gets mad if I'm not there when he needs me. They'll never forgive me for lagging behind, as it is." Then she charged forward, stumbling on the shallow steps as she went.

"*Ciao,*" Tristano called after her.

Carrie did not reply. When she regained her balance with what she hoped was some grace, she broke into a run. What a time to be a klutz when she had planned to make such a poised exit. The *Principessa* would think she was a gauche country girl: it did not matter what Tristano thought.

But when she caught up with the three men

85

as they sauntered behind a screening hedge of clipped cypresses, Carrie knew she was lying to herself again. It mattered, and it mattered a lot what he thought. However hard she tried to get him out of her mind it just did not seem to work. The least she saw of Tristano Cavalli the better. Thank goodness she need only endure his rather supercilious gaze today while they worked at the Di Monde villa. Supercilious had been the right word for it this morning, she decided in annoyance, there had been no warmth, no affection to his expression, just a handsome face which assumed a fitting air of superiority to suit the occasion of a morning canter with a *Principessa*.

However, on their return journey to the hotel that evening, Carrie was to learn that escaping Tristano was not going to be as easy as she had thought. They drove through the lengthening shadows of a long golden twilight. She was just relaxing against the plush upholstery of the Prince's limousine and thinking how pleasant everything was, when Ed Stern dropped his bombshell.

"Well, Carrie, how do you like this luxury living?" he asked, sucking contentedly on his pipe. "It beats the office hands down, wouldn't you say?"

Carrie smiled. "Sure does, Although, I

don't think I'd get much work done if we had to work in a showplace all the time. I spend too much time admiring the objects d'art."

Ed chuckled at her confession. "I admit that's hard to ignore. Isn't that a fabulous place? I could name a dozen men back home who'd give their eyeteeth for a chance at purchasing." He removed his pipe from the corner of his mouth, gesturing with it as he spoke. "I know this is going to break your heart, but I'm afraid you're just going to have to learn to live with a bit of luxury for a while longer, Carrie."

"What do you mean?"

"We're stopping at Villa di Monde for at least a week. Tim's got some great ideas for renovation and construction. The Prince isn't too sold on them at the moment, but I know he'll come round once he gets used to them. And for that to happen we need a little more time. When he invited us to stay for a few days I accepted without blinking an eye. It was a Godsend. Just the breather we need."

The singing of the tires on the smooth-surfaced *autostrada* made an irritating background noise which warred with the only thought Carrie managed to find screaming through her head. Another week! How could she stay another week, she thought in absolute panic, not with him living next door. She would see him every day now that the Venetian home had been vacated for the summer. It was an impossible arrangement; one she could not begin to accept.

Aloud, Carrie said, "I can't stay here another week."

"Why not?"

"My family are expecting me home." It was such a lame excuse that Carrie knew as soon as she said it that Ed would sweep her reasons away with his customary assurance while he convinced her it was no reason at all.

"Heck, Carrie, a telegram will take care of that. What about you, Tim? Any objections?"

"Not a one. In fact, I might grow to like this place after all," Tim said. And while he spoke he nudged closer to Carrie on the back seat, his leg pressing hotly against hers.

Repelled by his unspoken advances, Carrie edged closer to the door until the arm rest cut into her hipbone.

"I really would like to go home. Couldn't you manage without me?" Carrie asked, her voice coming out muffled and strange.

"What's the matter? Aren't you feeling well?" Ed's brow was furrowed in immediate concern.

"Not really. It must be the heat," Carrie mumbled, as she shrank into the gray leather upholstery desperately casting about in her mind for a reason for going home. It would have to be a very plausible excuse for Ed Stern to buy it. After a few moments she realized there was no valid reason for leaving. And as she could not bring herself to tell him her objections were because of Tristano's continued presence, she would have to go along with their plans. If she deliberately snubbed their Italian business contact, her rudeness would be apparent. So if she stayed she would have to fake continued goodwill toward the handsome Italian. How good an actress she would prove to be under the circumstances, Carrie would have to wait to see.

"More than likely it's the food. The Italians aren't as particular about cleanliness as we are," Tim commented in his usual Tim style. Then, peering closely at Carrie's pale face, he added, "Say, you don't look good."

"I'm sorry you're not feeling well, Carrie, but I really do need you," Ed explained, his face grave. "The typing is beyond me. And neither one of us takes shorthand. I suppose I could get a local girl, but heaven alone knows if she could understand me, or me her."

"It's okay. Don't worry about me. I'll manage."

"Sure, when we're settled in over there, things will seem better. This is such a change from what you're used to, you're bound to be upset. Just take it easy for a while and you'll feel fine. We'll get you a nice cool room where you can do your typing. Heck, if you're not up to packing, the hotel maid can do it for you."

"That's not necessary. After a good night's sleep I'll be right as rain," Carrie said with a confidence she did not feel. Tim was gazing soulfully at her, until she wanted to push him away to end the unsolicited attention.

"Hey, didn't you understand?" Ed asked, baffled by her answer. "We're going to the villa tonight. We're only going back to the hotel to pack. As a matter of fact, the Prince offered to have his man get our things, but my papers are such a mess, I couldn't trust anyone else to pack them."

So that was that! Carrie tried to still her pounding heart. Why hadn't she made a stand and insisted on returning home tomorrow morning as they had intended? Yet she already knew the answer to that question: Ed relied on her. That was why he had asked her to accompany him to Venice in the first place. And, whatever her personal feelings about the trip, she could not let him down.

While Carrie slowly repacked her suitcase the muted sounds of guests talking, and footsteps going up and down the staircase beyond her door, filtered inside the room. Fortunately her drip dry wardrobe was not in its usual state of soggy despair and could be safely packed inside her case. While a few days ago she would have been thrilled by the opportunity to become the guest of the prince and princess at their luxurious country villa, at the moment the idea was most unappealing. Perhaps she could hit it lucky and find Tristano otherwise engaged during her stay. Under those circumstances the visit could be managed with the minimum discomfort. But something told Carrie that Tristano would not be content to allow things to rest where they were. His very nature precluded any thought that their stormy relationship could stay suspended, as it were, on that fog shrouded bridge. He would renew his pursuit, if only to humiliate her further, or to prove to her that he could not be cast aside so easily. And the realization made her heart grow heavy.

Carrie stood with Ed and Tim while they waited for the water taxi. Behind her the recently vacated hotel glowed with welcoming light, appearing so friendly and comforting, that Carrie would have loved to go inside and let the other two go on without her. But she knew that was a childish idea of escape from unpleasant problems which must be faced. Flight served no purpose. The heavy evening air was warm on her bare skin. Several of the waiting tourists suggested the heavy dampness might be the forerunner of a storm.

A few minutes later, as they boarded the vessel, a brilliant flash of lightning shot through the sky to give authority to the assumption.

"Hey, I hope we don't get a soaking," Tim said, glancing apprehensively at the dark sky. "I don't trust that driver on such a winding road in broad daylight, let alone in a rainstorm."

"It doesn't smell like rain. These storms can linger about for days before they finally break. We'll be okay," Ed dismissed, while he checked one final time to make sure all their luggage was aboard. He gave a nod of assent to the hotel porter who exchanged a few hurried words with the boatman before waving him on his way.

As she looked back to the brightly lit hotel, Carrie felt tears stinging her eyes. The hotel grew ever smaller over the foaming wake of the craft until it gradually receded in the distance.

The Prince di Monde's driver awaited them at the landing stage. Once more Carrie rode the now familiar route in the comfort of the Prince's luxurious limousine. It was strange that she should feel so downcast while she was in the middle of such opulence. Her stomach pitched and her head ached until all she longed for was a darkened room and a nice soft bed. In fact, Carrie eventually dozed on the journey so that the hour long drive seemed to be accomplished in a matter of minutes.

"Hey, come on, Carrie. Wake up."

Blankly she looked up to find Ed Stern shaking her shoulder. To her surprise, when she glanced through the window, she saw the landscaped garden of the Di Monde's villa. They had arrived.

While Ed and Tim waited for their host, Ed insisted Carrie should go straight to her room and lie down. A maid came forth to show her to the upper floor.

While they walked up the broad marble staircase, the atmosphere of a silent museum was heightened. Here all was deserted. A pleasantly cool breeze swept through the open windows, filling the long corridors with sweet night air. At the deep windows thin white draperies fluttered and billowed with every gust, as if somebody stood behind them. A heavy carpet softened their steps on the marble floor, the red plush ribbon stretching ahead down a seemingly endless corridor.

"If you are tired, *Signorina*, you can have

your meal brought to your room," the middle-aged maid suggested in perfect English. She had noticed the dark shadows under her guest's eyes and was aware of the young American woman's dragging steps.

"Oh, would you do that. I'd be so grateful."

"It will be arranged at once. Is the *signorina* not feeling well? Would you prefer a light meal instead?"

"Very light. I guess something about the water must have upset me," she added lamely, knowing some explanation was expected.

"Ah, yes, that sometimes is the case. Perhaps tomorrow you will be recovered," the maid assured her as she unlocked a door at the end of the corridor. "This is your suite. Will you be working here also?"

"Yes, I'm sure I shall. I've got a lot of typing to do. Do you think you could make sure I have all I need?"

"Very well, *Signorina*."

Carrie followed the maid inside the vast room. It was even larger than her room at the hotel and its sheer luxury made Carrie gasp in delight, despite her current despondency. The bed was draped with yards of mushroom colored satin, the long folds of material attached to a circular canopy suspended from the ceiling. The bed itself was painted gold with an oval picture of cherubs set in a panel

94

on the footboard. There was a companion picture adorning the headboard, which had a molded design of fruit and flowers in a gilded streamer across its top.

"It's so beautiful," she gasped. "Do thank the *Principessa* for me."

The maid beamed in pleasure. "My mistress thought you would like this room. It belonged to her daughter when she was at home. *Signorina* Marta would be your age, *Signorina*, so I think my mistress has a soft spot for you because of that. You must remind her of her daughter."

Carrie absorbed this new information with surprise. No one had said so, but she had gained the impression that the Di Mondes had no children. Somehow the thought of the children's toys and clutter did not fit in with the sheer luxury of the villa.

"Shall I run a bath for you?"

Carrie gladly accepted the maid's suggestion. Perhaps a cool bath would perk her up. While the woman sang an operatic aria, screeching above the gushing taps, Carrie walked about the room where she examined the numerous art objects on the tables and admired the exquisite furnishings.

A delicately carved dressing table matched the bed. Two large, satin upholstered chairs were placed invitingly on either side of an

95

elaborate stone fireplace, which in this warm month was camouflaged by a huge gilded metal fan, of exquisite workmanship, the screen spread to its fullest extent to hide the blackened hearth. Before the screen was a tall vase of blue iris. The carpet was mushroom coloured to match the bed hangings. The only brilliant colour in the room was a deep rose satin couch which perfectly matched the brightest shade of the paintings. Carrie discovered the ceiling was also painted with flowers and baskets of fruit grouped about a central picture which echoed the theme on the bed panel. It was an exquisite piece of interior decorating.

When the maid had left, Carrie undressed and went into the bathroom. A white toweling robe hung on a hook behind the door. This room had the same rose pink in marble fittings complete with gold plated taps. A huge beveled mirror ran the length of the room. The light fixture was a deep gold filligree lantern which hung on a heavy old chain directly above the mirrors.

Carrie felt almost like a princess herself, as she stepped into the warm bathwater. On a glass shelf above the pink tub was a vast array of toiletries with very high priced names. Feeling deliciously wicked, she selected a carnation scented oil in a cut glass decanter and lavishly splashed the pink oil in the water. Then Carrie lay back to soak in the perfumed pink sea.

Sometime later while Carrie was toweling dry, a discreet knock sounded on the outer door. Her meal had arrived. Carried called to the maid to ask her to put the tray on the table.

When she finally emerged from the bathroom, swathed in the *Principessa's* complimentary bathrobe, Carrie found a tray bearing her meal. Between two silver covered dishes was a small bottle of champagne, a glass, and a crystal vase with a single long stemmed rose. While she was carrying the tray to the couch, she noticed a small folded paper tucked under the base. It proved to be a note from the Prince.

"Welcome to my home, my dear *Signorina*. This perfect rose is a mirror of your complexion. Sleep well. Bruno."

Carrie smiled as she read the brief message. Given such short notice, it was probably the best he could manage. The Prince must have intercepted the maid on her way upstairs. Surely the *Principessa* was aware of her husband's amorous intentions; yet she appeared to overlook them with an almost maternal indulgence?

There was a delicate omelette stuffed with

cheese and finely chopped tomatoes, and a cucumber salad. And though Carrie had thought she was not hungry, the food soon disappeared. The champagne made her throat tickle. More than likely the champagne was also with the Prince's compliments.

The more she thought about Bruno and his obvious intentions, the more cheerful Carrie began to feel. Tomorrow she would have to face him in person which would be far more of a challenge than reading secret notes. Still, armed with the knowledge of Bruno's intended seduction would make it easier to handle him. Forewarned was forearmed. If she must encounter Tristano at the villa, Carrie hoped it would be when the Prince made a play for her and she seemingly was receptive to his invitation. To think she was receptive to another man's advances while repelling his own would drive Tristano out of his mind.

Carrie chuckled aloud at the thought of his blazing anger. It would serve him right to discover he was not as irresistible as he thought. Yet what if he did not react as she expected him to? Once she gave Bruno encouragement, he would increase his pursuit. That was something she had not reckoned with.

Setting the tray aside, Carrie went to the

windows and lifted the heavy satin drapes. The moon was high in the dark sky, shedding a beautiful silver light over the lawns and bushes. The sound of horse's hooves came thudding along the path and Carrie wondered who could be riding at this late hour. A shadow suddenly fell across the lawn and Carrie's heart lurched as she thought she recognized Tristano. Her commonsense told her the rider could have been anyone, yet in her heart she was convinced he was Tristano. For all Carrie's anticipated delight in his anger, a part of her cried out to be with him out there in the moonlight.

She flung away from the windows. Who was she kidding? Every part of her ached to be with him. Despite the fact she was contemplating a flirtation with the Prince in order to rouse Tristano's anger – or was it more out of revenge? – she wished there was no need for the charade. Her heart went with the mysterious dark-haired rider as he cantered across the rolling grounds to the adjoining villa. The worst thought of all was who might be waiting for him when he got home.

CHAPTER 5

The first morning of working at the Di Monde villa passed so pleasantly, Carrie was glad she had not risked causing a scene with Ed by insisting on going home. The *Principessa* had gone out of her way to make her feel at home. After breakfast she had sent a large bunch of fragrant roses to Carrie's room. A working desk had been outfitted for her beside the windows: there was a surprisingly up-to-date electric typewriter, reams of paper and all the pens and pencils she would ever need. Carrie had discovered it was a pleasure to work in such luxurious surroundings. Working at the villa was beginning to make her feel like an elegant society reporter on assignment. She had even successfully managed to thrust the disturbing picture of Tristano to the back of her mind.

Lunch was another delight. The *Principessa* suggested she share the meal with her while the men finished their discussion. The meal was served on the terrace beneath a brightly striped awning. It was like being at a luxury resort having her lunch served outdoors on a flower decked terrace. The only thing missing in the picture was a swimming pool.

"Will you ride with me after lunch?" the *Principessa* asked while she offered her guest a second helping from a vast bowl of salad.

"I'd love to, but I'm afraid I didn't bring any riding clothes."

"Don't worry about that." The Principessa smiled at her.

"No really," Carrie protested, "I've got a pair of knit slacks but they're hardly for riding."

"My daughter was about your size. We surely have some of her riding things around."

All her objections were swiftly dispelled. Now the ride was a foregone conclusion, Carrie found she was looking forward to it. She finished her lobster, declined a second glass of white wine.

"You are wise. One needs a clear head for riding," the *Principessa* said, as they went inside the villa. The stables were a miniature of the villa and so grand did they appear, at first Carrie thought them to be another house. The *Principessa* chuckled in delight at her mistake and she quickly recounted the amusing story to the young Italian groom who joined her in laughter. Their laughter was not unkind, however, and Carrie did not feel hurt by it. As she stood breathing in the scented

101

warmth from the garden while the groom saddled their horses, Carrie wondered what the folks at home would think about this. If only they could see her now. No one would believe she had gone riding with a princess, nor that she had cut such a dashing figure in her elegant riding attire. The borrowed britches fit a little tight, for Marta must have been slimmer in the hips than she, yet they were a lovely cut and the buff fabric was as soft and pliable as fine velvet. A casual blue cotton blouse of her own seemed a suitable companion to the breeches. Riding boots had been more difficult to obtain. At last a pair had been produced from somewhere; the forgotten possession of a former guest who luckily had feet as large as her own. The shiny black boots completed her illusion of wealth. Carrie had never felt so indolently rich and high class before in her entire life.

The *Principessa's* mare was sleek black with beautiful lines. The mount chosen for Carrie was a fine gray mare with a sweet and gentle face. The *Principessa* assured her guest that the animal was gentle and trustworthy. At this welcome news Carrie relaxed somewhat, for she was unsure of her riding prowess after several years absence from the saddle.

Carrie found to her surprise she was able to manage the horse quite expertly as they slowly cantered down the drive and turned towards the lake road.

"How old is your daughter, *Principessa?*"

"Twenty-four . . . or she would have been," came the surprising answer.

"Would have been?"

"My Marta was killed several years ago."

Carrie gasped at her clumsy mistake. The *Principessa* placed a cool thin hand on her arm to assure her that her daughter's death was no longer a painful subject. "Ah, think nothing of it. You weren't to know. It was an unfortunate accident. Now I know why this side of the lake is called the unlucky shore. Our neighbors too have suffered their share of tragedies. It is . . . how you say . . . a curse . . . *malocchio* the evil eye, or so our ancestors believed. Today we must say that is nonsense, yet sometimes it makes one wonder."

Carrie grew increasingly uncomfortable when she reviewed her *faux pas,* yet how was she to know Marta was dead. The neighbors' misfortune to which the *Principessa* referred must have been the Conte Cavalli's crippling accident.

Before them the lake shimmered silver in the sunlight as the breeze rippled the water into metallic waves. Though the *Principessa* had continued to make small talk, their former easy relationship had grown strained.

103

Knowing she was the one who had unwittingly spoiled the mood made Carrie feel guilty. As she silently followed her hostess along a rocky track which wound around the lake, Carrie was aware of the intensity of the sun beating down on her bare head. They moved beneath stately cypresses and tall umbrella pines which though they afforded some shade, their uplifted branches allowed the golden sunlight to stream through unimpeded.

A man's voice hailed them. At the sound Carrie's stomach lurched with apprehension. She knew it was Tristano. Had this innocent ride been a ploy on the *Principessa's* behalf to bring them together?

The *Principessa* waved to him as she reined in her mount. And a few minutes later Tristano joined them on the narrow road. Today he was more casually dressed in a yellow short sleeved knit shirt, the sleeves clinging to the well developed muscles of his upper arms where the tanned flesh had the appearance of a sculptured figure, so perfect did it appear.

"Well, when they told me you were out riding, I didn't believe it," he said, a grin playing about his mouth as he saw Carrie's flushed face.

"The *Principessa* asked me to accompany her."

"I usually turn back here," the *Principessa* said, glancing down at her watch. "Besides, it's time for my *siesta*."

Carrie also began to turn her horse's head, but Tristano put a restraining hand on her bridle. "No, don't go back. There's a famous ruin a few kilometers from here. I'd like you to see it while we're out."

"Yes, *Signorina*, do go on. There's no need for you to go back. The locals are proud of their ruin. Go see it by all means," the *Principessa* urged, her face set in a strained smiled. "The old monastery is very picturesque."

"I've probably ridden my limit," Carrie protested, longing to go back in the safe company of another. "I should go back too." She grew alarmed as the *Principessa* began to move away, not waiting for her, clearly telling her she did not want her company on the return journey. The black mare's hooves slid on the loose rocks as the *Principessa* spun about to face them.

"Nonsense. Go with him," she cried, waving to Carrie. "Don't you know Tristano will sulk if you don't." Then with a final wave the *Principessa* increased the mare's pace as she galloped back toward the villa.

"Are you afraid of me?"

Carrie turned in her saddle to face him, her

105

face flushing at his remark. "Not in the least," she declared hotly.

"Then stop wasting time. Let's tour the ruin."

They rode side by side towards a curve in the road, each careful to keep their eyes averted from the other's face. Carrie was annoyed with herself for acting so flustered in his presence, yet he had taken her by such surprise she was unable to act as if nothing had happened. When Tristano appeared her composure always suffered a shattering blow. Today was no different, despite her grand ideas of ignoring him in the future; those thoughts were completely divorced from reality once he was here beside her. How she wished she could have greeted him casually, instead of being at a loss for words. Somehow the gay nonchalance she coveted was completely out of reach. Carrie stole a glance at his set profile, finding the arresting sight made her shudder. The yellow shirt emphasized his dark face, making him seem even deeper black in contrast to the brightness.

"Here's the monastery. They say it was destroyed in Charlemagne's time."

Carrie was enchanted with the scene before her. It would have made a perfect picture and she was sorry she had not brought a camera with her on this trip. The tumbledown yellow rock structure straddled the road. Curtains of purple and yellow trailing vines draped the crumbling surface, while a tall bank of rhododendrons, ablaze with myriad shades of pink blossoms, shielded the building from the lake. Behind the crumbling walls could be seen a stand of tall cypresses, straight as sentinels guarding the road.

"It's beautiful. Can we go inside?"

"Of course." He dismounted and assisted Carrie to the ground.

However had she steeled herself against his attraction, she was not prepared for the flaring heat she felt when he touched her, nor the trembling which began in her legs when he leaned close and she smelled the intoxicating scent of his shaving lotion mingled with the hot muskiness of masculine skin. Swallowing her discomfort, Carrie squared her shoulders and followed him through the masonry archway into a small courtyard floored in blue and white mosaic. Here the vines tumbled profusely over the interior walls and ivy and red honeysuckle tendrils fought for possession of the crumbling monastery. A cascade of blue wisteria drooped lazily over the archway.

Everywhere was so wild and beautiful, Carrie paused a moment to drink in the atmosphere. It was during this moment of peace that she realized the setting at the old monastery was too moving for her to be here alone with Tristano.

"Hey, come on," he called, waving to her to follow him.

"I was admiring the view."

"It's so lovely, but there's an air of sadness here too. I knew you'd like it." Tristano smiled at her when she came to stand beside him in the center of the courtyard. "Through here. There's more."

Obediently she followed him through a second arch and entered a dark, dank room which must have been a monk's cell, for the only light filtered through a vine screened slit high in the wall.

"I'm glad you like the *Principessa*. You seem to be getting on well with her. She's always been like a mother to me," Tristano said, his voice echoing in the empty space.

"Yes I like her and I think she likes me in return. I really put my foot in it today. No one told me her daughter was dead. I'd no idea."

"Marta drowned in the lake. She went swimming from the point. That's why the *Principessa* never rides this far, she does not want to be reminded," Tristano explained, his face growing serious as he spoke. "Marta was a wild girl. I suppose we all were wild

108

then. No one ever knew if it was too much to drink, or a cramp – suddenly I saw she was in trouble. Then I couldn't see her anymore."

"You were there!"

"I brought her out of the lake."

"Oh, how awful!"

"Yes, it was a great tragedy – we were engaged."

Carrie gasped with shock, her exclamation echoing round the small room. "I'd no idea," she mumbled, feeling ill at ease for having brought up the subject in the first place.

Tristano smiled slightly at her shock. "I'm surprised you didn't know. I thought the *Principessa* would have enlightened you. It was to be a momentous occasion: our families would have been joined for the first time in over four hundred years."

"Had I known I wouldn't have mentioned her."

"I understand that. Thanks for the sympathy, but I got over it long ago."

"Did you love her very much?"

Tristano turned towards her, his face in shadow. In the silent room his breathing was audible, his breath quick and shallow as if he was troubled by her question. "You surprise me by asking that. I would have thought you assumed I was incapable of loving anyone

109

but myself, or so you led me to believe the other night."

Carrie blushed. "Perhaps I shouldn't have been so mad at you," she relented, "but after me thinking there was something more . . . and finding you . . . I," she stopped, hating the idea of reopening all that was so painful to her.

Tristano touched her hair a moment, his face growing thoughtful. "You know, Carrie, you remind me a lot of Marta. Her hair was like yours, her features too. When I first met you I couldn't place the resemblance, but today it came to me."

"Is that why . . ." she began indignantly.

"Why what? Have you such little confidence in yourself that you think no one would be interested in you unless they imagined you were a former love?" he demanded angrily. "You never cease to surprise me."

Carrie stepped back, her own anger surging at his sarcastic criticism. Then the anger seemed to evaporate as Tristano put out his hand, his fingers tangling in her hair. This sudden change of mood alerted her to the danger of being in this isolated place with him. The discovery made her anxious to return to the sunlit warmth outside.

"Perhaps we'd better go," she suggested,

forcing her voice to remain calm, though her heart was pounding like a drum.

"Why? Do you want to run away because I'm getting to the truth at last?"

"Please, Tristano," Carrie began, but his hands came out to trap her and she did not resist as he drew her close.

"I have always admired you from the first because you are you. It is not because you remind me of Marta. There was no organized conquest as you seem to think, no grand design to my intentions. I find you attractive – until a couple of days ago I thought the feeling was mutual."

Carrie knew right then she should have moved away from him and escaped while it was still possible. She knew what she *should* have done, but she knew just as surely that she would not do it. His brown eyes were mysteriously veiled in shadows, yet their brightness seemed to penetrate the gloom as he inclined his head towards her. Then Tristano kissed her, his mouth hot and gentle against her own. There was none of that bruising mastery he had used after he captured her on the bridge, nothing to make her aware of his masculine dominance. And his tenderness made it harder than ever to resist.

She had allowed herself to soften in his

111

arms, was leaning against the hard strength of his body; this was so beautiful, such a magical enactment of all her dreams – then she remembered Gabriella. With an exclamation of dismay, Carrie jerked away from him. "What about Gabriella?" she cried.

"What about her?" Tristano repeated lazily, imprisoning her hands. "She's very lovely. Any man could be forgiven for kissing her. And I assume that's the damning scene you witnessed."

"Yes, I saw you kiss her, and I also heard that you and she are engaged!"

"Now where did you hear a silly thing like that?"

His sudden laughter succeeded in turning the last of her pleasure to anger. Carrie wrenched away from him and stepped backwards. "Does it really matter where I heard it as long as it's true."

Before Tristano could reply, Carrie was racing over the blue mosaic courtyard in the too tight riding boots, running and tripping over thick tendrils of vines which undermined the flooring. While she ran Carrie tried to resist an overwhelming urge to burst into tears.

"Wait, you little fool," Tristano cried, as he started after her. He caught her as she ran down the path towards the tethered horses who were placidly cropping the wild grasses beside the rhododendrum hedge.

"Let me go!" Carrie demanded angrily.

"Certainly." Tristano released her arms so quickly that she stumbled a moment on the uneven path before she could regain her balance.

"Let's get something straight," Carrie said fighting to control her emotion. "You are a good looking man who has dozens of women falling all over for you. I'll grant you that much. But can't you get it through your head this is one woman who's an exception to the rule? I've nothing against romance, it's just that I expect a commitment with it, a hope that it will lead to something more permanent in the future. You're not prepared to give me that. In fact, seeing you're virtually married to another woman, you're not free to make promises to anyone. You're just like Bruno. And why you should be so angry with him, I don't know, unless it's because he's stealing some of your thunder."

With that said, Carrie scrambled into the saddle and started down the road, leaving Tristano standing dumbfounded beside his horse. A few moments later she heard the thump of hooves as he urged his animal forward.

When he caught up with her Tristano

shouted, "Now you have that charming little speech off your chest, *Signorina* Neal I hope you're feeling much better." His face was thunderous as he spurred his horse and quickly passed her gray as he clattered along the lake path until he disappeared behind the shielding trees.

Carrie reined in and sat fighting for breath. Gone was any attempt at elegance as she slumped in her saddle in an ungainly heap. All the pleasure of the day had vanished. Those unflattering things were said, and whether they should have been, or not, remained a mute question. Now she knew she could write Tristano off for good. There was no way he would come back for another dose of that treatment. Tears slid from her eyes as she urged the horse forward and she trotted disconsolately beside the sparkling lake. Perhaps it was the weakening of her resolve to ignore his charm which had brought such a hasty condemnation from her lips. Carrie did not know what had made her leap at him with such ferocity, she only knew that she would never need to do it again. From the thunderous expression on his face as he galloped away Carrie knew Tristano would not bother her again. And that is exactly what she wanted, wasn't it? Miserably she was forced to admit it was not what she wanted. What

114

she really wanted had been about to take place in the dark room at the monastery. She wanted to feel his arms about her, to have his face close to her own and to taste the magic of his kiss.

Carrie walked inside the cool villa, glad to be out of the intense sunshine. Bruno met her as she crossed the black and white marbled floored entrance hall.

"Ah, did you enjoy your ride, *Signorina?* My wife is very fond of riding. Myself, I prefer other sports." His dark eyes flashed wickedly at the implication.

Carrie took a deep breath: It was now or never. If she was ever going to make this flirtation stick she would have to begin somewhere. Today, after her painful repudiation of Tristano's attentions, she felt least able to follow through with her planned flirtation. In her present state she was perhaps no match for Bruno's polished manner, yet she could not help clinging to the hope that it mattered to Tristano if she allowed the prince di Monde to pursue her.

"Thank you for the lovely rose," she said with a charming smile. "Have I you to thank also for the champagne?"

He smiled as he nodded in agreement. "Well, I thought a glass of champagne is just what was needed to bring the sparkle back into your life. You know, it's not hospitable for you to be ill the first night you are here. But as I trust you are feeling better today, you're forgiven."

Carrie smiled at him. "I'm completely recovered," she lied, finding this act was not as difficult as she had expected. "What a lovely home you have here. My room's more luxurious than I ever imagined it could be."

"Thank you for your kindness. These treasures have been in my family for years. Like my neighbors, I suppose we could open the villa to the public, but so far I've preferred to keep its pleasure for lovely guests like yourself."

Carrie modestly lowered her gaze from his bold brown eyes, growing uncomfortable beneath his unblinking stare. The Prince gently slipped his hand beneath her arm and he guided her towards the side terrace.

"Come, before you go upstairs you must join me for a nice, cool drink. I can see how hot and tired you are. Early afternoon's not really the perfect time for riding, *Cara*."

There, the first little endearment had been sneakily slipped into the conversation. Carrie smiled to herself. The endearment followed on the heels of his solicitous discussion of her wellbeing, and was accompanied by an urgent, yet gentle hand on her arm. Bruno

116

continued to gaze into her face with deep concern. The Prince's attentions would serve her well. After that brush with Tristano this afternoon he would be doubly amazed when she appeared to be falling under Bruno's spell. He would be amazed and violently angry.

They shared a glass topped table on the wide terrace where Carrie was thankful for the bright striped awning which adequately shielded them from the hot sunshine. Though he continued to converse politely, Carrie remained aware of Bruno's glance sliding surreptitiously over her tight fitting britches and of his well-manicured hand lying inches from her own on the cool table top.

"I really have to get back to work," she said at last, searching for an excuse to break up the little tete-a-tete. The *Principessa* must be taking her *siesta*, thus leaving the way open for her husband to pursue his amorous intentions. In the bright, revealing light, Carrie was surprised to see that even the Prince di Monde was not as young as she had first imagined him to be. More than likely his gleaming black hair was dyed to maintain its rich color. And though his waistline was still trim and his movements agile, there was an air of tiredness and strain about his eyes where fine age lines formed a network across his sunbronzed cheeks.

"Your boss and his assistant have gone next door for the next few hours to review plans for the Cavalli hotel," Bruno revealed as his hand slid towards hers to trap her fingers before she could draw away. "We are all alone. So there's no need to go back to slaving over your typewriter. Why not sit here and talk to me."

Not wanting to make a show of forcibly disengaging her hand from his, Carrie maneuvered to slide her hand free. He did not stop her. "I really must go indoors, the sun's very hot. Your wife's idea of a *siesta* sounds admirable. Even if I don't work, at least I'll lie down."

A gleam came to his eyes at her words. In alarm Carrie hoped the Prince was not interpreting her casual remark as an invitation to join her in her room.

"My poor wife feels the passing years; for her a *siesta* is a necessity. I take out a few hours for a quiet period of relaxation in the afternoon, but I do not sleep. To sleep away such a beautiful afternoon seems to be such a waste, don't you think, *Signorina?*"

Carrie purposely avoided his gaze, though she was well aware of the meaningful smile which spread over his face. "I thought a *siesta* was the custom," she began lamely, while she searched desperately for something to say.

118

The Prince laughed. "Who told you that? All Italy repairs to the bedroom in the afternoon, granted – but it is not always to sleep."

Abruptly Carrie stood, scraping her chair noisily over the stone steps. "Well, *Ciao*," she managed with a calmness she did not feel. The Prince stood also and now he was blocking her path of escape.

"Ah, but it would be too ungallant of me not to accompany you indoors," he said, his heavy eyelids lowered seductively to hide his deep brown eyes.

"Oh, that's not really necessary," Carrie protested, inching her way round the table.

"Ah, but I insist. By the way, did my wife forget to invite you to our party tonight?"

"She didn't mention it."

Bruno slid his arm about her waist, his fingers absently plucking at the back of her blue blouse as he spoke. "Poor Sophia, she's becoming absentminded. You must come to grace my party. I won't take no for an answer."

Carrie found his mannerism disconcerting as she felt the heat from his fingers penetrating to her skin. Now she was wondering what she would do with her erstwhile admirer once her room was reached. As the servants also appeared to be taking their *siesta*, she was

119

going to have to handle the situation without any outside help. While she always felt somewhat in control with Tristano, despite her own susceptibility to his charms, the aging prince, who was admittedly after thrills, was an unknown quantity. Would he try to press his attentions on her now that he assumed she was willing to go along with his flirtation?

These thoughts plagued Carrie as they walked through the ringing marble hallway. She was uncomfortably aware of the Prince walking beside her up the grand staircase, his hand resting lightly on her waist. When he did not press for any further contact, Carrie found her confidence returning. The feeling was reinforced when her door loomed ahead like a safe harbor in a storm.

"Thanks for walking me to my room, but it wasn't really necessary, you know," Carrie gushed, disentangling herself from his possessive embrace.

The door handle turned easily in her grasp. Carrie pushed the door open, alarmed to find that Bruno had stepped closer and she felt his hand flick out to stroke her cheek.

"Yes, by all means get some sleep. My parties usually last well into the night. I insist on dancing with you at least until midnight."

Surprised and relieved that he was not going to press her further, Carrie almost ran inside her room after bidding him a hasty goodbye. Once she had closed the door, she listened a moment to make sure he was actually going to leave. She was soon rewarded by the sound of the Prince's departing steps. At the sound Carrie breathed a huge sigh of relief as she flopped ungracefully on the mushroom satin coverlet. Wow! that was close. Playing the coquette required a certain amount of finesse. If the Prince had insisted on coming inside her room she would have to have repelled him, failing that she would have had to shout for help from the staff thereby causing a nasty scene. Either way it would have been the end of her invitation to stay at the villa. Though the *Principessa* was probably aware of her husband's philandering, in having the fault brought to public attention one would not earn her favor.

With a great sigh of relief, Carrie pulled her swollen feet out of the tight riding boots and she dangled her legs over the edge of the cool satin spread. A lovely cool breeze was wafting through the open windows and she sighed with contentment. She had not asked who else would be at the party, but she had a sneaky suspicion Tristano would be there. In fact, he seemed to be almost a permanent fixture around here; whether it was merely because he was their closest neighbor, or whether it was because he had almost become a member of the Di Monde family, Carrie did not know.

She had no choice but to wear the ecru party dress again, though it reminded her unpleasantly of the party at the Santi *palazzo*. The emotion came back with such force, it made her stomach pitch. It would be an exciting change to attend a party at this grand villa. While the Santi party had been magnificent, she had felt too much of a stranger to really enjoy it. At least here she had been made to feel at home. She was in fact a house guest of the Di Monde's and would probably be introduced as such. That vital difference would give her an added boost of confidence. Besides, the Prince had promised to be very attentive. If she could just manage to keep him comfortably at arms length without having to come to a showdown with him, she would be able to sit back and watch Tristano's reaction at leisure.

Rolling onto her stomach, Carrie watched the filmy white draperies fluttering like sails at the open windows. Then a disquieting thought came along to rob her of her satisfaction: What if Tristano did not care whether she encouraged the Prince di Monde or not?

CHAPTER 6

Later that evening Carrie nervously approached the lighted ballroom where the French windows stood wide to admit a cool breeze sweeping from the lake. She had taken great pains with her appearance and she knew she was looking her best. The music and laughter of the party had already penetrated the comparative calm of the upper floors. And by the appearance of the driveway, which she had glimpsed from the window, Carrie rightly assumed a large crowd had already arrived. The sea of black limousines and brightly painted sportscars proclaimed the wealth and social standing of the Di Monde's party guests.

When she walked inside the ballroom, which was a blaze of lights, the *Principessa* came forward to greet her. Tonight the *Principessa* di Monde wore a flame colored dress with floating sleeves and about her thin neck gleamed a heavy necklace which Carrie knew was not set with rhinestones.

"How lovely of you to come, my dear," the *Principessa* said, as she gave Carrie a light embrace. "Let me introduce you to someone who is most anxious to meet you."

Carrie turned in surprise to find a girl of about her own age hovering in the background. The girl had luxuriant dark hair and her lovely, dark-skinned face seemed vaguely familiar, though Carrie knew she had never met her before.

"This is Lucia Cavalli ... Tristano's sister."

Now Carrie knew why she thought she had recognized the stranger. That arresting family likeness wrenched her heart, however hard she tried to ignore it. Lucia had those same large, liquid brown eyes, surrounded by dark curling lashes, and that arrogant, high cheekboned face with its prominent nose. Surprisingly the same features which made Tristano a handsome man, had been scaled down to the appropriate degree to make his sister an equally beautiful and alluring woman.

"How do you do, *Signorina* Cavalli."

"No, you must call me Lucia," the girl protested, with a lovely smile which revealed perfect white teeth set in a frame of dusky, wine red lips. "I so much have wanted to meet you, Carrie."

The *Principessa* smiled warmly at the two young women and she whispered, "I'll leave you alone to get better acquainted. The

124

refreshment table is over there." Then the *Principessa* turned to greet a party of new arrivals.

The dark haired Lucia led Carrie to a green velvet chair set invitingly before the open windows. Tristano's sister had such a voluptuous figure, that Carrie felt almost schoolgirlish beside her. Lucia's magenta gown was modestly cut, yet it could not camouflage her ample curves.

A maid came to them to offer a tray of filled champagne glasses. They both took a glass and settled down to talk.

"Did your brother tell you about me?" Carrie asked curiously.

"*Si*, and though he likes you, I'm afraid he does not approve of women working."

"I gathered as much."

"He is obvious, no? Well, though I love him very much, Tristano is too much like our father. Papa thinks a woman's place is in the home and that she should not be allowed to leave it without her husband's permission."

"Like being in Purdah."

Lucia laughed in delight at Carrie's comparison. "Exactly . . . oh, they are what you American call . . . Chauvinists. Is that the right name?"

"Yes. That's what they sound like to me. But I thought you were studying art in

Florence, surely that's leaving home."

"Studying yes, working not so good." Lucia sighed and she put down her empty glass. "You must tell me how you began work, Carrie."

"Well, after college I took a secretarial course. Then, when this job opening came along, I grabbed it. That's about all. My family were thrilled to have me earning my keep."

Lucia smiled. "Oh, you make it sound so simple."

"For me it was. And necessary. I'm afraid my family don't own a fabulous villa or a stable of thoroughbred horses, or fleets of luxury cars. We live in a modest frame house on the edge of town and everyone has to work to make ends meet. Perhaps if I had your advantages, I wouldn't be so anxious to go out to work. I kinda like this taste of luxury," Carrie revealed truthfully, finding Lucia was very ease to confide in.

"Oh, pleasant though those things are, I admit, they do not make up for having your own identity." Lucia leaned forward, an earnest expression on her pretty face. "Though we have only just met, I feel as if I've known you for years. Can I confide in you, Carrie, for frankly, I've no one else here who would be in the least bit sympathetic."

The other girl's confidence took Carrie by surprise, as did the gesture when her small, perfectly manicured hand gripped her own excitedly. "Sure, Lucia, confide all you want."

"I have a chance for a wonderful job in Rome!" Lucia revealed breathlessly. "Oh, it's the most exciting chance ever. It's just what I've always dreamed of. I will be sketching fashion designs for a leading magazine. I was so ecstatic, I nearly flew home to tell him, then . . ." Lucia paused, her face clouding and she glanced down at her feet. "He said no."

"He? Your father?"

"Oh, not Papa, he's an invalid these days and has little to do with the running of the family. No, it is Tristano who makes all the decisions for me. He says it is not possible for a Cavalli to accept such a job."

"Why not?" Carrie snorted, her anger freshly roused at the thought of poor Lucia having to sacrifice such a fantastic job because the lordly Tristano thought it beneath her. "Many well-to-do families take jobs these days. It's not for the money, but to give them a purpose, to be able to do something creative and satisfying."

"Oh, that's right. That's why I want to take this job, Carrie. I knew you would understand," Lucia cried, clasping Carrie's hands in her own. "Even if the job was totally with strangers – the magazine owner is a family friend. Will you do a big favor for me?"

"Sure, speak up," Carrie encouraged her, though she had a sinking feeling in the pit of her stomach. It did not take a mind reader to know what favor the lovely Lucia was going to ask of her and Carrie was not sure she was equal to the task.

"Please, please speak to my brother for me. Let him understand too what this means to me. Tell him just the way you said it then . . . about how much it means to be creative. I want to be something, not somebody. All my life I've been the Conte's debutante daughter, but now I want more. I want to be me – Lucia Cavalli. There is so much here to offer the world." Lucia dramatically struck her heart, her dark eyes rolling expressively as she poured out her emotions to Carrie's sympathetic ears. "I have a lot to offer, though I know it isn't modest to say that."

Carrie gripped Lucia's hand, feeling terribly maternal as she saw the other girl's large brown eyes flood with tears which she fought to keep under control.

"Don't worry. I'll see what I can do," Carrie offered, though she felt defeated before she began. After the couple of run-ins she

128

had experienced with Tristano, she would be lucky if he spoke to her again, let alone heard her out in so personal a matter as the topic of Lucia's job.

"I knew you'd be my best friend. The *Principessa* is very dear, but she comes from another age. Then young women of quality did not seek employment, nor did they disobey the wishes of their father or their brothers. She's just too old to help me, though inside I think she wishes she too could have had a life of her own when she was young. The Prince is a terrible husband, you know."

"Yes, I guessed as much," Carrie agreed, glancing to where she could see Bruno dancing the *Bossa Nova* with a willowy young thing in crimson chiffon. "Your brother may not listen to me, Lucia. In all truth, I can't say our relationship has been exactly smooth."

Lucia laughed at Carrie's admission. "No, from something he said I gathered that you were not as easily maneuvered as he is used to women being. Ah . . . he was in such a black mood this afternoon . . . so black that I . . ." Lucia's voice trailed away as she watched her brother stalk arrogantly inside the ballroom.

Carrie turned to watch him also and she caught her breath at the stirring sight of Tristano in powder blue evening dress with an elaborate frilled shirt which made him look like a riverboat gambler. She had to admit that he looked magnificent. Lucia's revelation made her feel guilty; Carrie knew she was the cause of Tristano's black mood. The argument they had at the ruin must have made his day.

"Perhaps I'm to blame for his bad temper," she admitted uncomfortably. "We had a few words this afternoon. Sorry if it made things difficult for you, but your brother is . . . well, he's . . ." Carrie was unsure how to explain the situation to his sister. She need not have worried; Lucia knew her brother as only a sister could.

"He is domineering, arrogant and hopelessly charming. And he also thinks all women are put on earth for his entertainment," Lucia described accurately. "Oh, you need not tell me about my brother. So angry was he at my suggestion, he even refused to let me act as guide at the villa," Lucia revealed sadly. While she spoke she twisted her hands together in agitation. "That is something even Papa allowed me to do to earn a little of my own money for school expenses. Tristano says no. He thinks the exposure to the public has been bad for me and has made me want even more freedom."

"Perhaps when he calms down he'll change his mind."

"Don't bet on it. Tristano's generally a man of his word."

"Yes, I should have guessed that much." Carrie turned in her chair just in time to see the Prince di Monde, with a definite predatory gleam in his eye, heading her way.

"Oh, I see Bruno has his eye on you." Lucia giggled. "Fortunately I'm safe from his clutches. Though he's a wolf he respects the sister of his friend."

Carrie smiled at Lucia's statement and she wished she too could be assured of the Prince's respect, yet she did not suppose that same regard would be extended toward the secretary of his business associates.

"Ah, the two most beautiful women in the room," the Prince said, as he kissed Lucia's hand. When he reached for Carrie's hand she purposely kept it at her side and thwarted his intention. "Now, *Signorina* Neal," Bruno continued, undaunted, "I've come to claim that dance you promised me. It's long overdue."

Carrie knew she could not delay the start of tonight's charade any longer. Bruno had been promised a dance and she would make it one to remember, for to her immense satisfaction she had seen Tristano heading this way. As the orchestra struck up a lively number Bruno gripped her hand, his fingers hot

131

and demanding as he imprisoned her in his firm grasp. After bidding a hasty goodbye to Lucia, who nodded understandingly, Carrie found herself whisked to the center of the vast dance floor. The prince was a good dancer, being light on his feet and decisive in his actions. To her surprise Carrie found the ordeal was far more pleasant than she had anticipated, her pleasure being vastly increased when she saw Tristano's dagger sharp glances of disapproval as he scowlingly watched her performance.

At the first opportunity he came forward and cut in.

"The young lady's mine now, Bruno."

Laughing, the Prince reluctantly allowed Carrie to be swept away. A moment later she saw him dancing with the willowy girl in crimson chiffon.

"Well, are you pleased with yourself?" Tristano demanded, pulling her so tight against his chest it became difficult to move.

"Pleased?"

"Yes, for creating such a stupid spectacle with Bruno."

"I was not a spectacle. We were dancing, much as you and I are dancing at the moment," Carrie reminded him with icily controlled anger.

"Well, whatever you choose to call it you

appeared foolish. Bruno is old enough to be your father."

"So."

"So you should not be flirting with him."

"Dancing can hardly be called flirting."

"What about sitting on the terrace. Allowing him to come up to your room."

Carrie felt her face reddening. "Who told you that?"

"It doesn't matter who told me. Is it true?"

"Well, not in the way you think. He did walk me to my room after we'd shared an innocent lemonade on the terrace. But he didn't come inside. That's just what it was – a completely innocent . . ."

"Bruno never does anything in innocence. You should have learned that by now," Tristano snapped as he steered her towards the doorway.

"Where are you taking me? I want to dance."

"I don't. I want to try to talk some sense into your pretty little head, though why I bother is beyond me."

Carrie tried to pull away from him but Tristano kept on dancing. It was infuriating, but he managed to keep perfect time to the music all the way across the black and white marble floor and out onto the terrace. Like a movie set they danced from the gloomy entrance hall into brilliant moonlight which flooded the bushes with silver. Carrie's heart was thumping with anger and dismay when at last Tristano stopped moving and he pulled her wrists together as he tightly imprisoned her.

"No you stay here and listen to me. You surely must be aware that girls who invite Bruno to their rooms get themselves talked about."

"I did not invite him. He followed me there. And I closed the door on him like a good girl. You would have been proud of me," she finished sarcastically as she managed to regain some of her composure. "Anyway, even had I chosen to invite him inside my room, I can't see what business it is of yours."

Tristano snorted his disgust. Letting go her hands, he reeled away and leaned against the chill wrought iron railing bordering the terrace steps where he remained until he had mastered his temper. This unreasonable anger he was experiencing was becoming more difficult to contain with each fresh confrontation. Carrie was a totally infuriating woman.

"While you are here in Venice you are my responsibility. For that reason alone, I have an interest in your actions. Besides, I know what an unprincipled wolf Bruno can be."

"There's nothing else behind it?" Carrie gasped in surprise as his matter of fact statement caught her off guard. She had hoped his anger was caused by wounded affection; to have him dispel that hope in such a thorough fashion made her heart lurch.

Tristano hesitated a long moment before giving his answer. "No, there's nothing else. Did you think there was?"

"No, of course not. Why should I think that?" Carrie dismissed with a nonchalance she did not feel. Instead grief welled to her throat. Surely he could have at least made an effort to excuse his rash behavior on the grounds that he cared for her. That is the reason she would have expected from a playboy like Tristano. What a blow to her self-esteem to hear him plead his reason for warning her off Bruno. It was as if by his statement he was telling her she was not worth getting angry about, not worth challenging another man over . . .

"Bruno's bad news for you. You forget how well I'm aware of your old-fashioned romantic ideas. Love and honor are not words in the Prince di Monde's vocabulary. You can take it from me."

"As someone who should know," she snapped as she tossed back her hair defiantly.

Tristano caught his breath at her angry

words, but he mastered his surprise in time to mutter through clenched teeth, "This is my last attempt to save you from his clutches, I just wanted you to know he discourages easily if you know the right words. Or perhaps you'd like me to tell him."

"I don't need any help, thank you. Bruno is quite charming. And, as I am here at the villa for a mini-vacation, the least I can do is avail myself of the local color," she said, trying to sound sophisticated. And, by his angry frown, Carrie assumed she had succeeded.

"Oh, yes, he's quite a local sight. Well, lots of luck."

"Thank you."

As Carrie stepped towards the open windows Tristano called her back. "I saw you talking to Lucia earlier. She seems to like you. I'm glad."

Carrie paused beside the open French window. Yes, everyone appears to like me but you, she noted mentally. Aloud she said, "How strange to hear a compliment from you. Yes, I think Lucia's a lovely girl. And you are making a big mistake."

Tristano's eyes narrowed as he sensed what was to come. "Mistake?"

"By not allowing her to take that job in Rome."

"Oh, now I get the picture. You are to

intervene on her behalf. Forget it."

"Well, poor Lucia didn't know how famously we always get along when she asked for my help," Carrie added sarcastically.

"And whose fault is that? You can't say I haven't tried to be pleasant."

Carrie smiled at his statement. "That's one way of putting it. Anyway, Tristano, however we feel about each other personally does not affect Lucia. She really needs this job, and though you don't approve of women working, why don't you give her a chance?"

"And why don't you mind your own business," he snapped, turning on his heel. "She's my responsibility, not yours."

"Why can't you let her be her own responsibility? Surely she's old enough to know what she wants."

"What a person wants is not always what is best for them."

"Oh, that's a stupid statement, if I ever heard one. She's right. You are against women's rights, against their very existence except as something to be chased and caught," Carrie exploded in anger.

"You are a foreigner and you don't understand Italian family life. My sister comes from an old and noble family. It is not permitted for her to take a paying job. Besides, she has no need . . ."

"Oh, you're so wrong! She has a need inside herself. She longs to be someone. Just being the daughter of the Conte Cavalli isn't good enough. Because you're a man given all the privilege of that sex, you can't begin to understand how worthless she has been made to feel by your rejection of her ideas. She was allowed to nurture a talent for which she's found an expression, but now you're denying her that expression. They wouldn't have offered her the job if they hadn't thought she had the ability to carry it off. Give her a chance."

"Are you quite through?" he asked, a sarcastic smile lifting the corners of his mouth. "You must have taken public speaking in school."

"Stop trying to slide out of this," Carrie cried, annoyed by his attitude. "Lucia's entire future is at stake and you're trying to make me look small."

"This is my problem, not yours," Tristano snapped.

"You're wrong," Carrie cried, clenching her fists in frustrated anger. "It's *Lucia's* problem. And you won't listen to her."

"All right, I'll rephrase that to say it's *mine* and *Lucia's* problem. We'll solve it to suit ourselves, thank you."

"To suit you, is more like it," Carrie

snorted, her anger bubbling uppermost until it threatened to explode. There he stood, a dark immovable shadow etched against the moonlit terrace, so set in his archaic ideas, so totally unyielding to her suggestions, she might as well have been talking to one of those marble statues in the hallway. "Not letting her take the job is bad enough, but to stop her working as a guide is the last straw."

"Oh, you think so?"

"Yes, I do."

"Why?"

"By taking away even the job her father allowed her to have, you've crippled her self-confidence. Can't you see that?"

"All I can see is a spoiled, very rich little girl who's no idea what the real world is like. They'd slice Lucia up in little pieces on her first day. She's just not prepared for all the jealousy and back stabbing she'd find on a Roman magazine. Despite the fact we know the owner, she will be working on her own merits if she takes the job. Can't you see, Carrie," here he stopped to reach for her hand, but Carrie kept her hands tightly locked behind her back. "Can't you see I'm not just trying to dominate her? I want to protect Lucia. After a few weeks of that pace she'd be so disillusioned, so hurt ... she's too dear to me to allow that to happen,"

Tristano defended hotly as he stepped out of the shadows.

"That's only an assumption. Why don't you let her try it? Lucia might surprise you. And anyway, you didn't answer my question about her identity, about . . ."

"Listen, Carrie Neal, I'm tired of answering your questions, tired of discussing things with you." Tristano gripped Carrie's wrist in a bone-crushing grasp. "I intend to do what I feel is best and I'll do it without any prompting from you. In future just stay out of my business."

"It will be a pleasure! In fact, I'll go you one better than that, I'll stay out of your life," Carrie cried, wrenching away from his strong hands.

She fled towards the darkened hallway, not pausing until she reached the ballroom entrance, half expecting him to be in hot pursuit, she was surprised to find him still on the terrace, his tall figure casting an elongated black shadow over the windows. He was not even going to bother to come after her! The realization was like a bucket of ice water on her emotions.

Tears misted her eyes and Carrie rapidly blinked them away. Through the blurring water haze she saw the winking lights of the ballroom and she could hear the lively music throbbing through the palatial rooms of this lovely villa. There was a party going on and she intended to be part of it. What did it matter that Tristano was simmering out there on the terrace? It was stupid of her to have thought she could intercede with him on Lucia's behalf, in the first place. Yet, because of the dream she had cherished about his secret feelings for her, Carrie had thought she might be able to accomplish a miracle.

Holding her head high, Carrie stepped towards the bright lights. Perversely she had discovered she loved him even when she fought with him. Why did he try to dominate her too? She almost expected it where Lucia was concerned, for Tristano took his position as head of the household seriously. But though his forceful behavior roused her ire, when she looked at him and remembered what it felt like to be held by him, or to taste the sweetness of his mouth on her own, Carrie found her animosity flickered to a warm ember of love. What a crazy situation she was in: she was in love with a man who roused her to anger whenever she set eyes on him.

"There you are, *Cara*. What kept you so long?" Bruno was at her side, his arm sliding around her waist. And he glanced pointedly at her deep v-necked bodice as his eyes probed the secret under the soft ecru fabric. Even

141

when he knew he had been discovered, Bruno continued unabashed. "Come, I'll bring you some *hors d'oeuvres* and a big glass of the best champagne."

"Thanks. I could certainly use a drink," Carrie said, raising her voice for Tristano's benefit. As she talked to the Prince, out of the corner of her eye she had noticed that distinctive blue suit moving amongst the party guests. No one else had a suit like that; nor could any other man match Tristano for physical beauty, Carrie added treacherously. The admission made her heart throb in misery. She could have had Tristano on his terms which, looking back on it now, may not have been all that bad; instead she had tried to impose her own rigid ideas on him and thereby she had lost all chance of earning Tristano's love.

Like a wooden doll, Carrie followed where Bruno led. From somewhere close by a woman's musical voice carried clearly, the adoring words shattering the very last shred of Carrie's composure.

"Tristano, darling. There you are! Where've you been all evening? Why, *Caro*, you know you're the only reason I'm here."

The laughing voice belonged to Gabriella. Carrie turned to watch the lovely princess swooping down on Tristano, her tall, elegant

142

figure swathed in yards of white crepe which fluttered in the breeze. The white fabric leant an air of fragility to Gabriella's appearance turning her lovely face angelic beneath a coronet of honey blonde hair all sparkling with diamonds. To Carrie's anguish she watched Tristano slide his arms about Gabriella's back while he planted an affectionate kiss on her pink tinted cheek. Not content with such lukewarm affection however, Gabriella seized his face and gave him a thorough kiss on the mouth. The depth of his feelings for the other woman were visible as Tristano's hands stole toward Gabriella's shoulders where he dug his fingers into her flesh, his suntanned hands a violent contrast to the ethereal white fabric. A round of applause greeted Gabriella's bold actions. When Tristano released her he turned to make a laughing bow to the other guests.

A few minutes later Carrie watched them walk towards the darkened hallway. When Bruno reappeared with a plate of fancy party snacks and a glass of sparkling champagne, Carrie's appetite had flown. From where she was sitting she had an unobstructed view of the driveway, and though she did not want to watch them, she could not prevent her gaze straying towards the handsome, fairy-tale couple who were embracing in the moonlight. For what seemed an eternity the blue and white fabrics were blended in a fluid, breeze stirred marriage until at last the man and woman parted.

Carrie had to crane her head to see what they did next and she no longer kidded herself that she did not want to watch. She must watch for she was lured on by a morbid fascination to know what they did. Gabriella opened the door of a low slung white sports car and she ushered Tristano into the passenger's seat, then she started up the engine of the powerful car. A moment later they crunched down the driveway, with Gabriella accelerating as they approached the gate leading to the highway. Soon the white sports car and its glamorous occupants had disappeared into the moonlight, and Carrie was left alone with her tortured pictures of their embrace.

But she was not alone! A hot touch, a whispered endearment, and she was uncomfortably reminded of the Prince di Monde's presence. This was the man whom she had intended to use to spur Tristano's jealousy. She had encouraged Bruno, but to what purpose? Though she might convince herself Tristano had lied when he said his warning about the Prince was merely out of a sense of responsibility, whatever lies she told herself could not erase that vivid memory of

144

him kissing Gabriella. Tristano was gone and she was left with her aging admirer, who thought himself entirely welcome because of her lack of resistance to his advances.

"Come, dance this one with me, *Cara*. This slow dance is played just for us," Bruno breathed down her ear, his hands sliding up her arm.

"I . . . I've . . ."

"Come." Given no further chance to formulate an excuse, Carrie was swept towards the dance floor where the couples were barely moving to the slow, romantic music.

Lifting her head, Carrie forced a smile as she blinked back her treacherous tears. Smile, you fool, she told herself contemptuously, you're dancing with a prince!

CHAPTER 7

The employees of Stern and Associates breakfasted at eight on the patio overlooking the formal gardens. A warm fragrant breeze caressed Carrie's hair, but she felt too ill to appreciate it.

"Well, Carrie, that was some party last night," Ed said, while he scraped his spoon jarringly against his cereal bowl. "You seemed to be having a ball."

Carrie smiled sheepishly at his comment, then she winced as she moved her head too rapidly for it was pounding like a bass drum. Too many glasses of the Prince's best champagne had given her a king size headache.

"I didn't see you dancing much," she managed casually as she picked half-heartedly at her scrambled eggs.

"That was probably because you were too busy being the star of the show," Tim remarked sourly.

"Oh, Tim, don't be dumb," Carrie said quickly, looking down at her plate to hide her discomfort at his reminder.

"Carrie's of an age to have fun. Don't fault her for it. I'm sure everything was quite harmless." Ed carefully tamped his pipe, then he lit it and puffed reflectively. "I don't suppose you feel much like getting down to work today with that hangover."

"Oh, I'm okay. I can still type. I'm not that badly off."

"Great. We took some more estimates yesterday afternoon. I've had them sent up to your room."

The estimates were a task to decipher for Ed's scrawl read like Greek. Carrie realized Ed had needed her yesterday when she had been riding beside the lake with the *Principessa*, and the acknowledgment brought a wave of guilt. Had she been along to take shorthand notes as she should have done, he would have been spared all this extra work. She resolved to spend no more hours frittering away her time while she pretended to be something she was not. This luxury life could get the better of you at times until you almost began to think it would go on for ever, instead of remembering to keep it in its proper perspective. Yet what was a proper perspective?

Carrie dropped the sheaf of papers on the desk and restlessly she crossed to the windows. Outside the bright sun shone warmly over the brilliant, tropical hued flowers in the border below the terrace. Last night she had danced continuously with Bruno. And, after a number of glasses of champagne, she had allowed him to kiss her. That he was an expert at the task, she had no doubt. Carrie knew she did not feel any affection for him, yet the Prince di Monde promised instant glamor which last night had suddenly seemed to have been snatched away. She had needed to be told how lovely she was, how desirable, how she made his heart palpitate with passion. And, for a little time, she had even allowed herself to believe him. Bruno was cagey in his pursuit, for even now he still allowed her freedom instead of pressing her to greater intimacy. Though Carrie knew he was cleverly maneuvering for the kill, she appreciated the fact that he had not insisted on a conquest there and then. Last night, with her reason for encouraging the Prince already gone from the party, she had no choice but to continue with her flirtation. To her surprise she had found Bruno's attentions had not been hard to take, for this was the first time she had been romanced by a prince, and though he was undoubtedly an experienced wolf, his line was highly flattering, nonetheless. Sheer flattery on the road to possession is the game he played. And once she had succumbed to his wiles, Carrie knew he would move on to new, more challenging victims.

Impatient with herself for allowing him to make a fool of her, Carrie flung away from the window and forced herself back to the typewriter. There was no sense in wasting any more time in daydreams. She had the Prince and she did not want him: she wanted Tristano, but she did not have him. What a mixed-up situation this Venetian spring was turning out to be!

Carrie was further humiliated when she saw Tristano crossing the entrance hall later that morning. He was dressed for riding.

"Aha, I trust your head is not too painful this morning? I was told you downed a lakeful of champagne," he remarked, his mouth curled in a sarcastic smile.

Carrie blushed hotly at this comment. "I'm feeling okay."

"Great. Perhaps you'll come for a ride with me."

"No, not now. I've got a lot of work still to do."

"Is Bruno coming by for a little afternoon drink? I'm sorry, I didn't intend to interrupt your rendezvous. How unthinking of me."

His sneering tone made Carrie increasingly annoyed, though she fought to keep her emotions under control. If she lost her temper he would have gained exactly what he wanted. "No, Bruno's not coming by. I told you last night . . ."

"I know – everything's innocent. I haven't forgotten. It's just that I don't believe it."

"Well, whether you believe it or not, it's true. Anyway, after last night's spectacular little love scene on the dance floor, I shouldn't think you'd mind. At least Bruno and I have been discreet."

"Aha, so you're admitting now that it's Bruno and I," he cried, his face darkening in anger. "What I do, as I've told you before, is

149

none of your business. Gabriella is impulsive. There was nothing behind it."

"Ha! Now it's my turn not to believe the story. Though perhaps you don't know it, I also saw your touching embrace in the moonlight – and Gabriella driving you away."

Tristano caught her arm and pulled her about to face him as Carrie threatened to run away.

"Listen, Carrie Neal, you're not my guardian. I do what I want. And it's not open to your censorship. Gabriella and I are old friends."

Carrie glared at him as she jerked her arm free. "Well, you're certainly welcome to your old friends. If you ask me, Gabriella deserves you."

He laughed as he stepped towards the terrace. "Do you want to repeat that for her? She's out here . . . Gabriella."

"I'm going back to my room. It's safer in there."

"Shall I tell the *Principessa* you won't be joining us for lunch?"

"You can tell her whatever you like," Carrie flung as she raced up the staircase. She was rewarded by the sound of his mocking laughter echoing up the stairwell.

The remainder of the morning was a disaster. Carrie made mistake after mistake in her typing, and she erased and crossed out more than she put down. She was so disgusted after an hour of this that she felt like throwing the work through the window. To add to her inattention she kept hearing Gabriella's laughter floating up from the lawn where she was playing croquet with Tristano and the *Principessa*. The three beautiful ones must be waiting their lunch which was probably being served on the terrace. Carrie knew she could not join them after her heated words with Tristano; worse still, perhaps Gabriella had heard them also. The thought made her feel lonely and very humiliated. As the minutes ticked by she felt even more wretched. Carrie finally crept downstairs, hoping the three people on the terrace would not hear her, or in that case she would not be forced to join them or appear rude.

The sky had clouded over and apparently afraid of a rainstorm, the *Principessa* must have ordered the meal to be served in the conservatory, for the terrace was deserted. When she listened Carrie could hear their voices drifting from the palm bedecked room at the rear of the house. It was a pleasant surprise to find she could have the terrace all to herself. She walked outside for a breath of air, but the thundery weather was so oppressive everywhere was still.

The impending storm was making her head ache again, and Carrie felt thoroughly hot and uncomfortable. If drinking too much champagne made her feel like this, she made herself a promise never to overindulge again.

When the maid noticed her seated on the terrace, she came outside to ask if she would like to be served here, or if she preferred to join the others in the conservatory. Carrie said she would have a salad and a fruit cup out here on the terrace.

To her dismay, when the food arrived, it was Bruno and not the maid who was carrying the tray. At the unexpected sight of him, Carrie gulped, embarrassed as she reviewed his probable thoughts concerning her after last night's abandoned behavior. She had let him hold her too close and she had danced with him too often: even worse than that she had not stopped Bruno when he had whispered endearments in her ear, not when he playfully nibbled her neck. After such encouragement he must be ready to close in for the kill.

"Dear *Signorina,* allow me to serve you." Assuming a very serious expression, the Prince served her from a chilled salad bowl cradled in a bed of crushed ice; then he poured her a generous glass of white wine, totally ignoring her feeble protests concerning the alcohol. When the meal was served, he pulled out a chair and prepared to join her for lunch.

"Thanks for bringing my food, but I really shouldn't drink anymore, especially after last night," Carrie protested, as she cut into her chilled melon.

"Champagne and white wine have totally different reactions. Besides, if you drink a little wine, perhaps you'll be persuaded to be kind to a man who is totally devastated by your charm." Bruno winked at her while he spoke.

Carrie was beginning to grow uncomfortable beneath his scrutiny. And she was also freshly embarrassed each time she recalled their more intimate encounter last night.

"You really must excuse what the champagne made me do. I assure you I don't usually ... well, I don't let men kiss me."

"Nonsense. A woman like you is born to be kissed."

This was not going to be easy. "I mean men I don't know," Carrie finished quickly.

"You know me now."

It was hard to avoid that very intimate smile he flashed her as he smoothly dismissed all protests.

Carrie managed to forestall his handclasp,

however, for she was in time to see his beringed hand sliding quickly over the tabletop. At that precise moment she picked up her knife and fork to keep both hands occupied. Uttering a sigh of irritation, Bruno pretended he had been reaching for the salt thereby smoothly concealing the incident. He was just too cagey for words and Carrie found he was more than a match for her.

"Listen, Prince di Monde . . ."

"Bruno."

"All right, Bruno – last night was a lovely party. There was a lot of champagne, a lot of laughter – the music was romantic . . ."

"All in all it was a wonderful evening."

"Yes. I enjoyed myself, but . . ."

"But! Now what a terrible word that is. Surely you're not going to say you already regret the lovely time we spent together." His eyes turned soulful as he spoke.

Carrie gulped in dismay, and she acknowledged she was facing a master. Short of telling him to get lost, she was going to have her work cut out to dissuade him from this flirtation. Why didn't she flat tell him to get lost? The argument that he was her host was no argument at all. And she certainly could not say she wanted his attentions. Was it because she still clung to the hope that she could make Tristano jealous by flaunting the

154

Prince's attraction for her? Miserably Carrie admitted the latter came the closest to the truth. By still clinging to the remote chance Tristano cared for her secretly, her future decisions would be made accordingly. That was the reason she did not tell Bruno to leave her alone. Until she knew, without any doubt, Tristano was indifferent to her actions, Carrie intended to string the Prince di Monde along. Taking a deep breath, she launched once more into an explanation of her actions last night. It would be too awful if he thought she was madly in love with him!

"Though as I said, I enjoyed last night, there was no more to it than the party atmosphere . . ."

"If you think I'm going to accept that, you are very wrong, *Bellissima*," Bruno interrupted as he tilted the wine bottle to refill his own glass. When he proffered the bottle to Carrie, she indicated her first glass of wine still untouched on the table. "Whether it's a misguided sense of modesty which makes you make such a preposterous statement, I don't know," Bruno continued while he treated her to an indulgent smile. "There was too much magic between us for me to accept such outrageous lies."

Carrie stared at him in dismay. The man was just not going to take no for an answer;

he was as bad as Tristano in that respect. You could certainly call Italian men determined, if nothing else. "Seeing that your wife . . ."

"Sophia?" The Prince seemed genuinely surprised by her latest objection and he breathed an audible sigh of relief when he understood how flimsy was her objection to sharing a love affair with him. "If that is all you are worrying about, my dearest *Signorina*, you must put that thought completely out of your head. Like most Italian wives, Sophia is a model of understanding. She allows me a certain freedom in these matters, as she should. And she bears you no ill will, I can assure you."

"That's exactly the way I want to keep it," Carrie blurted, glad at last to have something she could turn to her own advantage.

"And so you shall," Bruno soothed, his smile as cunning as a wolf. "Why should she not continue to love you? We have done nothing to cause her pain. We danced. We kissed a little, but what is a kiss today, *Bellissima?* No, you are far too concerned with unimportant things. You must promise me you will think no more about these silly objections to what promises to be a lovely relationship."

While she listened to his husky, heavily accented voice, Carrie could almost imagine she was watching a movie where the continental charmer was about to snare his unsuspecting victim. Bruno was absolutely incredible! "We come from different worlds. I'm not used to parties and glasses of champagne. I live simply."

Bruno smiled as he digested her latest statement, and he patted her hand assuringly. "Of course, I understand exactly what you are trying to say to me. Rest assured, our friendship will continue in the same pleasant way."

Though his assurance was delivered so convincingly, Carrie knew she should be wary. "I hope so. I wouldn't like to think you got the wrong ideas about me."

"Ideas? Now what ideas would I have about you?" Bruno chuckled at his thoughts. "You must relax and enjoy yourself. There is no party tonight, so your evening will be your own. There is something I want to ask you. A favor."

"Sure."

"Will you do me the honor of touring my little greenhouse? There it is." He turned in his chair and indicated a white painted glass and wrought iron gazebo on the lawn beside the lake. "There I have a collection of exotic plants. There's one very beautiful flower, my own variety, which I have named in your

157

honor, Carrie – it's true," he said, when Carrie protested his statement. "When you are far away I will have that exquisite bloom to remind me of my lovely Carrie."

She gulped at his flattering words, finding his tearful expression so immensely moving, despite her inward knowledge of its falsity. He was so good! Had she not known the Prince for what he was, she would have been convinced his heart would ache unconsolably once she was gone. "That's very nice of you," Carrie mumbled, realizing she must make some response. "I've never had a flower named after me before."

"Now your name will go down in history," Bruno assured, as he lowered his eyelids seductively over those knowing brown eyes. Now at last she was caught unawares and his hot hand imprisoned hers on the table top. "Promise you'll come with me tonight."

"What time?"

"We'll take a little stroll after dinner, if you'd like."

"Okay. I'll enjoy seeing your plants. Just think, a Carrie variety. That's really something."

What would Tristano think of this latest development, she thought smugly. He had constantly assured her Bruno had only one thing in mind where she was concerned, yet here he was, genuinely interested to the extent that he had named a plant after her. If only she could tell Tristano about it, yet there was no way she would be able to subtly inform him of her discovery. These past days he seemed to be informed of her every movement, so perhaps his informant would tell him of the latest startling development when she went to visit the gazebo with Bruno. Though the visit would be in all innocence, Tristano would probably attach great significance to their rendezvous. The fact she was going to admire a plant would be scornfully discredited. Carrie felt warm with pleasure as she pictured Tristano's black anger when he made the discovery of her tryst with the Prince. Whether he cared for her or not, at least she would be able to get even with him for his overbearing direction of her life. By forcing Tristano to admit she too could have an admirer would also make her even with him for his conduct with Gabriella. The Prince di Monde offered her a way to make Tristano pay for all the things he did to drive her to distraction.

When Carrie and the Prince di Monde eventually left the terrace, a blue clad figure extricated herself from the shrubbery. Gabriella had overheard their conversation and she was beside herself with amusement over the arrangements. She could not wait to convey her startling discovery to Tristano so that he too could enjoy the humor of the most fantastic lie to date by Bruno, who was an acknowledged master of deception.

When Gabriella beckoned to him from the lawn, Tristano excused himself from the *Principessa* who said she was going upstairs anyway, and he walked down the shallow flight of steps toward Gabriella. In the harsh daylight he was surprised to find her features appeared hard, while the revealing sunlight exposed fine lines which had begun to creep into her face. The sight surprised him, for Tristano had always thought of Gabriella as being a perennial beauty. How disillusioning to discover she was just like the rest of them. And worse still, he was older than Gabriella. If she was beginning to show signs of aging, what of himself? Tristano felt a quick shiver of distaste at the thought, for he found it very distasteful to consider growing old. Here he was heading into middle age without any lasting relationship to lean on. Though he knew he could not expect to be the world's darling for ever, Tristano had never looked at his position in quite this light before. For a moment he allowed himself to dwell on treacherous thoughts of Carrie, who was a girl who sought promises for the future, promises which, until this past few days, he had been quite unable to consider. Now, to vow fidelity did not seem the terrible punishment he had always considered it. In fact . . . Tristano cast aside his worrying thoughts, becoming angry with himself for even allowing them room.

"What do you want?" he asked Gabriella, his voice gruff with impatience.

"You're not going to believe this – oh, I can hardly stop laughing. Whenever I think about it . . ." Gabriella broke off her speech as she erupted in a gale of laughter. Then she caught his arm and steered him safely toward the open lawn where they could not be overheard. "Come away from the windows, it would be terrible if the poor *Principessa* hears this."

Tristano glanced back to the terrace to see it deserted.

"She's gone indoors for her *siesta*," he said. "Now, what great secret do you have to tell me?"

"It's about Bruno and that silly American girl." Tristano felt his jaw tighten and his hands clenched when he heard Gabriella's laughing statement.

"What about them? I don't know if their latest actions are particularly interesting to me."

"Ah, you wait. This is interesting. In fact, it may be Bruno's biggest coup. You'll never

161

believe what I overhead him saying just a few minutes ago."

"I would have thought spying was beneath you," Tristano remarked tersely.

"Oh, *Caro*, don't be so unkind. I didn't set out to spy, but when he followed her outdoors, what could I do but listen. Bruno is always so amusing, especially when he's hot on the scent of some young innocent – you did tell me she was innocent, didn't you?"

"Yes. Come on, Gabriella, I haven't all day to play detective. If you've something to say, let's hear it."

Gabriella pouted over his impatient attitude, then she tucked her slim white hand beneath his arm and leaned close. "Bruno has named a flower after your little American friend," she revealed breathlessly.

Tristano slowly allowed his breathing to ease back to normal, relieved by the innocent content of Gabriella's great revelation. "A flower! Well, surely that's his business, isn't it? I can't see why you find that so significant."

"Oh, sometimes . . . you're as dense as she is."

"All right, go ahead and tell me the wicked interpretation you've attached to his naming a flower after a woman," said Tristano in an amused voice.

"Where does he keep his flower collection? Now tell me that."

"In that monstrosity, that oversized birdcage on the lawn," Tristano said with contempt. "Everyone knows that."

"Exactly. And, as it's set so far away from the house, it's the perfect place for a seduction, you ninny. If he lured a girl out there, no one would hear her cries of protest – if there were any."

Tristano frowned at Gabriella's interpretation of Bruno's schemes. As a woman of the world who had earned her apprenticeship under the tutelage of titled philanderers like Bruno di Monde, Gabriella probably knew what she was talking about. "Surely even Bruno wouldn't attempt a seduction in broad daylight," he said.

"Ah, but you see, *Caro*, he does not intend to use broad daylight. This little meeting will take place by romantic moonlight. He's arranged a tour of his 'little greenhouse', as he charmingly puts it, for after dinner. And this wonderful rare flower he has named after your friend, is supposedly the draw. You'd have been amazed how readily she fell for it. Though I must say, as far as lines are concerned, I've never heard that one before. Bruno should be congratulated for his originality." Gabriella chuckled at the

163

thought of the scene which would follow the greenhouse tour.

Tristano's face went grim at the news. "The little fool! You say she went along with him, knowing Bruno like she does?"

Gabriella shrugged. "He was so convincing. The poor girl probably suspected nothing more than a tour of his greenhouse. Hm, how delightful. Won't she be surprised! How I wish I could be in at the kill . . ."

"That's enough," Tristano snapped. "It's a cheap and sordid trick and I'd have thought something like that to be beneath even someone like Bruno."

"Nothing's beneath Bruno, you should know that."

"But with this girl. How could he?"

"Ha! You're beginning to sound like a maiden aunt, *Caro*. Where's your sense of adventure? The silly girl's over twenty-one. And that is legally old enough to look after herself."

"Thanks for the reminder."

Gabriella scowled at his baffling attitude. "Well, you're certainly not being any fun today, *Signor* Cavalli. The business world must be too much of a strain on you. Once you'd have thought this highly amusing."

"Carrie Neal's different from the women we know. If she wasn't, I doubt if she'd have accepted such a blatant assignation."

"Unless she *wants* to meet him there. You don't give her much credit for sense, do you?"

"Knowing Carrie she probably thinks it's a charming old world compliment from a middle-aged admirer."

"Now you sound like her father," Gabriella sneered, tossing her head in contempt. "If this is an example of your future humor, next time I'll keep my stories to myself."

When he heard her sharp retaliation, Tristano realized he was being unfair to her. Gabriella could not know the deep responsibility he felt toward Carrie, nor could she really credit the girl with being a genuine person who accepted as truth the compliments a man paid her. There was none of the sophisticate about Carrie and the lack of that quality made her even more attractive to him. "Sorry, Gaby," he apologized as he slipped his hand beneath her arm. He squeezed her elbow affectionately. "I didn't mean to sound so stuffy. It's just that I feel somewhat responsible for the girl's actions. After all, I was the one who suggested Bruno as a client. Even knowing how outrageous he can be, I allowed her to become a guest at the villa. Perhaps we should nip it in the bud by telling the *Principessa*."

Gabriella laughed at his choice of words.

"Don't spoil the fun. Besides, I don't think we ought to involve the *Principessa* in this, do you?"

"I meant in a joking way, nothing more. Then he would have to show Carrie the flower and forgo the rest. It's too hard to generate a great romance when your wife is breathing down your neck. Even Bruno draws the line at that."

"You're right, yet it would be too cruel to tell the *Principessa*. Really, I think the least she knows about the Prince's activities, the better. That stupid girl should know better. Why should we have to rescue her. She got herself into this, now it's her problem to get herself out."

Tristano frowned as he spoke. "Perhaps you're right."

"I am. You know I'm always right about things."

"You needn't remind me of it so smugly."

"You men need regular reminders. Without them you become insufferable."

Laughing, they walked indoors and headed for the cool marble floored hallway on their way to the *Principessa's* private sitting room.

"The gazebo has lights, doesn't it?" Tristano asked.

"Of course. How else can she see the *flower*," Gabriella dismissed scornfully. "I know, if you're so interested in protecting your little friend's virtue, you can watch the gazebo from your balcony. Once Bruno turns off the lights, you can sprint over here and throw the master switch. Now wouldn't that be the story of the year! Everything would be fully illuminated in there. Now, *Caro*, if you intend to follow my plan, do let me know. I want time to bring a group of friends to watch the show. Wouldn't Bruno be the talk of the town for a while then?"

Tristano joined her in laughter at the outrageous suggestion, but his amusement lacked the necessary humor. He was sure Gabriella's proposal had been made in jest, yet the basic idea appealed to him. It would be far better to be at the Prince's villa, however, than have to sprint over the adjoining lawns to rescue the little idiot.

"If you want to go on to town, I'll give the *Principessa* your regards," Tristano suggested, as they paused at the foot of the staircase.

"Would you? I really must rush off. I'm having a fitting at three and I can barely make it now. Heavens, I hope this weather holds, I can't imagine an outdoor fete in the pouring rain."

"For you, my angel, I'm sure the heavens will restrain themselves," Tristano promised, as he pressed a fleeting kiss on Gabriella's soft cheek. *"Ciao,* Gaby."

Gabriella paused in the doorway to wave goodbye to him before she hurried outside into the sunshine.

Tristano leaned against the curved bannister and reviewed their conversation. The idea of revealing Bruno's duplicity still hovered in the back of his mind, yet it seemed unnecessarily cruel to hurt the *Principessa* by revealing such unpleasant details. Though he doubted she was ignorant of her husband's romantic encounters, Bruno was generally discreet. If Carrie had acted as sensible as she fondly imagined herself to be, this situation would never have happened in the first place. Of all the little fools to lead Bruno on to this point! He felt like wringing her lovely neck.

Scowling at his perplexing thoughts, Tristano quickened his steps. As Gabriella said, none of this was any business of theirs, for had she not accidentally overheard their conversation, no one but Bruno and Carrie would be any the wiser. For a moment he wished he had not known about the rendezvous, then he immediately dismissed the idea. He knew, and he was going to do something about it; just what, at the moment, he did not know.

From the back of the house came the sound of voices. Without a doubt one of the voices belonged to Carrie; in his current mood Tristano could not face a confrontation with her. If he were forced to speak to her at this moment he would say all the wrong things, and perhaps a number of things for which he would be very sorry. And taking the steps two at a time, he sprinted up the staircase to the *Principessa's* sitting room.

CHAPTER 8

Throughout the evening meal Carrie was aware of an underlying current of excitement in Bruno's manner. Observing this, she began to have second thoughts about the innocence of their rendezvous later tonight. It was not unusual for someone to be so eager to present a flower, that he could not concentrate on either the conversation, or the meal. In fact, had Tristano not been a guest, she knew she would have casually mentioned to the *Principessa* this new variety of flower which her husband had so generously named after their guest. As it was, with Tristano glowering at her every time she caught his eye, Carrie decided to keep her mouth shut. More than likely if she said anything he would have some scathing comment to make, or worse still he might laugh sarcastically at the very thought of anyone wanting to name a flower after her. As it was she must endure his black looks. Yet perhaps his anger was because his spy had revealed her intentions. In that case he would be dealt another blow when the spy reported she had kept her rendezvous with the Prince di Monde.

Their antagonism toward each other was so marked that the *Principessa* looked from one to the other in surprise. It was clear some rift had taken place between them.

"Do have some desert, *Signorina* Neal," the *Principessa* urged in an effort to interject some conversation into the now silent meal. And she indicated the large ice cream bombe in the center of the table. The dessert was a special creation of a master chef who had given the recipe to their cook. It was a delectable three tiers of pink, green and chocolate ice cream all lovingly wrapped in swirls of whipped cream and dotted with candied fruits and nuts.

"Oh, no thank you," Carrie declined regretfully. "The veal parmigiana was so good, I've no room left for dessert."

Just then the Prince caught her eye and winked. Carrie's hands grew clammy and her knees began to shake when she realized he had misinterpreted her statement to infer that she was breathlessly awaiting their meeting, and had not time to waste on food. Oh, boy, she certainly could have chosen her expression more carefully. Bruno really was unbelievably conceited over his charms. Almost as conceited as Tristano had been

"Did Gabriella have an appointment this afternoon?" asked the *Principessa*, turning her attention to Tristano. She felt obliged to at least make an effort at drawing out her guests, whether they wished to be civil, or not. In fact, this entire meal was spoiled by the hostility which bounced about the table. What with Tristano's black mood and the girl's nervous gestures, then Bruno would have to be in one of his abstracted moods. It really was unforgiveable of them all. The *Principessa* forced a smile to her tight mouth as she waited his reply to her question.

"Yes, she had a fitting with her dressmaker," Tristano said at last, forcing himself to be pleasant. "I told her to go ahead."

"Ah, yes, the months preceding a wedding can be so hectic," the *Principessa* paused, her attention focused on Carrie who was choking over her coffee. "Are you all right, *Signorina* Neal?"

"Fine, thanks," Carrie gasped as she fought back her tears. The uncomfortable choking

171

sensation had made her eyes water, but the *Principessa's* casual revelation had made the tears into an expression of grief. Now at least she knew the real situation between Tristano and Gabriella. For all he had falsely pretended they were merely good friends, the truth had been inadvertantly revealed. He was just hours away from his attempts at romancing her, while Gabriella amassed a trousseau for their wedding. How despicable could you get!

"Gabriella will make a lovely bride, don't you think?"

Tristano nodded, unable to find words to answer the *Principessa*. The sight of Carrie's red face and her obvious discomfort told him what she must assume. Before he was able to correct that assumption, Carrie had excused herself from the table. He could follow her onto the terrace, but he knew that action would only lead to an unpleasant scene.

After allowing a decent interval to elapse, Bruno put down his coffee cup and made a great pretence at nonchalence as he sauntered outside to the terrace. He had taken Carrie's exit as a cue; the girl's ingenuity had surprised him, for she appeared so naive about the correct steps to a flirtation.

In the distance the boom of thunder rolled in from the hills, the vibration tinkling the myriad crystal teardrops on the vast chandelier above the table.

"Oh, it's going to rain after all," the *Principessa* said, glancing apprehensively towards the sky. "This thundery weather really is too much. It always gives me a sinus headache."

"After such a muggy day a thunderstorm's only to be expected," Tristano replied as he turned his attention to the terrace. From where he sat he could only see Bruno. How he longed to walk outside and forestall their meeting, yet he knew he would not do that. He must stay to be polite to his hostess.

"Are you walking home now, or will you stay for a drink?" the *Principessa* asked as she got up from the table.

This was the excuse to leave that he had been waiting for. "No, I think I'll be getting home. I'm afraid stormy weather doesn't improve my disposition," Tristano excused as he held open the dining room door for the *Principessa*.

"Now don't make such silly excuses. It was obvious to everyone that all the thunder was not in the heavens. Have you and the little *Signorina* had a lover's quarrel?" she asked, smiling up at him with a frankly indulgent smile.

Tristano nodded, touched by the *Principessa's* concern. "We can't hide much

173

from you, can we?"

The smile faded from her thin face and she glanced over her shoulder towards the terrace. "No. Yet some people have never learned that, after all these years. Goodnight, Tristano. Will you come over for a ride tomorrow morning?"

"Yes. The same time. Goodnight."

Impatiently Tristano waited in the shadowed hallway while the *Principessa* walked upstairs, her figure making an erect pillar of blue as she gradually disappeared in the gloom of the upper floors. She knew. Bruno had never fooled her with all his stories and his pretence. Now Tristano was glad he had not broached the subject of her husband's assignation in the greenhouse. This was something he intended to settle by himself.

When Tristano stepped out on the terrace, he found it was deserted. And there, moving across the lawns was the pale blurr of a woman's dress as Carrie walked beside Bruno to the gazebo. Tristano was suddenly struck by an awful thought: in all his anger over Carrie and Bruno, in all his scheming to keep them apart, there was one fact he had never fully explored; Carrie may not be the foolish innocent he and Gabriella supposed her to be. What if she actually welcomed Bruno's advances?

Carrie found the humid night air as uncomfortable as a steam bath. There was barely a breeze so that even the normally fluttering leaves on the tall poplars were still. As they crossed the lawn a great jagged flash of lightning bisected the dark sky, so suddenly did it appear, that she gasped aloud. A moment later a companion boom of thunder rolled and echoed over the lake like a round of artillery fire.

"Ah, we must hurry. I wouldn't want you to get drenched," Bruno said, taking this opportunity to link his arm through hers on the pretext of hastening their steps.

"Perhaps we should turn back," Carrie ventured apprehensively as the wind suddenly picked up and began to swirl her thin skirt about her legs.

"Nonsense. I promised to present you with my special creation tonight and tonight it's going to be, storm or no storm." Bruno smiled at her in reassurance, an odd, indefinable expression crossing his face. "Perhaps we'll be trapped inside the gazebo until the rain stops," he suggested, drawing her arm more tightly against his body.

"Maybe it won't rain," Carrie said, plucking up her courage. What a stupid nut she was being. She was quite able to manage Bruno, despite his formidable

175

reputation, there was nothing to fear. The vast glass enclosed gazebo offered a perfect view to onlookers. In fact, so public would the interior of the gazebo be once it was lit, she sincerely doubted if Bruno intended to do more than show her the flowers.

After this brief inner lecture, Carrie found she had confidence in her ability to handle matters. She felt so much better, in fact, that she was able to look over the lovely landscaped gardens and appreciate its forlorn beauty as the storm rapidly approached. The trees began to whip about like large black creatures, their twisting shadows weaving a design over the lawn. Unfortunately her goodwill lasted only until she dwelled on what had transpired at dinner. The *Principessa* had unknowingly answered her most burning question. There was no longer any doubt that Tristano and Gabriella were engaged to be married, despite his amorous behavior. Though why inconsistency should surprise her, she did not know: here was the Prince di Monde married for many years, a man old enough to be her father, embroiled in the throes of what promised to be a perfect conquest.

"Ah, here we are," Bruno said as he reached for the doorhandle.

At close quarters the gazebo appeared much larger than Carrie had supposed it to be.

The building was two stories high. It looked like a monstrous elaborate birdcage made of white painted wrought iron interspersed with dozens of windows. When the Prince switched on the light the interior of the building was flooded with white fluorescent light. Now she could distinguish palms and wooden planters overflowing with tropical foliage standing amid rows of brightly colored flowers. Paths of red crushed rock divided the different species of plants.

"What do you think of my little hobby now?" the Prince asked, pleased when he saw her great surprise.

"It's all so professional looking. This whole place looks like a nursery, or some horticultural exhibit. I'm really impressed," Carrie exclaimed as she stepped towards a table of nursery flats filled with wine and white striped begonias. Behind this tray was a tall box of gloxinias in the most brilliant shade of blue she had ever seen. "Now I recognize those, but what kind is my flower?" Carrie said innocently as she glanced expectantly about the gazebo, growing impatient to see her namesake.

The room was ablaze with colors, the air thick with the combined scents of leaves and damp earth mixed with the faint perfumes of the different flowers. Though the Prince had told her it was a greenhouse, up until this moment Carrie had not been wholly convinced of the innocence of his suggestion. When she looked about the orderly tables of plants a vast wave of relief crept through her limbs. He had only intended to show her his plant collection after all. And to think how much she had sweated this out. Tristano would definitely read more into the entertainment, however.

"Your flower as you so charmingly put it, is inside here."

Eagerly Carrie followed the Prince inside a small inner room which was filled with orchids. Their lovely colors were breathtaking and she felt as if she was smothering in a sea of pink, and yellow and lilac. The flower perfume was readily apparent in this enclosed space. It was a surprise to learn there were fragrant orchids, for the usual corsages of Carrie's limited experience had not been scented.

Bruno reached for a plant pot containing a lovely white orchid all spotted with pink and lilac and blue.

"Here, this is the Carrie orchid. Isn't it magnificent?"

Carrie gasped with delight at the lovely flower as she drank in the faintly spicy scent of the blossom. "Oh, I wish my family could see this. They'll never believe me in a million years. I don't suppose you've got a picture I could take back with me."

The Prince shook his head. "I regret to say there are no pictures. The technique of raising this exquisite bloom is my secret at the moment. Someday, when it is ready for commercial exploitation, there'll be pictures galore. Were it possible, you could have one of the blooms to take back with you, but I'm afraid it would be too fragile to stand the journey."

Carrie was too enraptured by the orchid to notice the Prince maneuvering behind her as he opened a small black panel beneath the wooden plant table. Overhead a fresh clap of thunder rolled and so violent was its echo, it seemed to shake this structure until Carrie was afraid the glass panes would shatter about their heads.

"Don't be alarmed. The greenhouse has weathered many a storm," the Prince assured with a confident smile. "Don't you think the flower is worthy of your pretty name?"

"The orchid's lovely," Carrie said, smiling up at him. "I'm honored that you would name the flower after me. Never in a million years had I dreamed of having anything named after me. How can I thank you for giving me such a big surprise. It's great."

Bruno smiled as he fleetingly touched her hair. "I'm sure we can think of a way for you to thank me, Carrie," he said huskily as he took a step towards her. He took the precious flower and gently placed it back on the shelf. Then, when he turned back towards her, Carrie saw a curious, almost menacing look on his face. "As a matter of fact, *Carissima*, I'm thinking of the most perfect way of all for you to reward me."

Carrie's hands began to shake as his meaning came through loud and clear. As she opened her mouth to protest, Bruno reached beneath the table and the gazebo was plunged into inky blackness. Carrie screamed in shock.

The Prince clicked his tongue in annoyance. "Look there, now the lights are gone. It must be the storm," he said, but the hint of laughter in his voice betrayed him.

Carrie was convinced it was not the storm which doused the lights. There must be a switch close at hand to turn them off. "You turned them out deliberately, didn't you?" she demanded, stepping away from him.

"Why do you say something stupid like that?"

"Now I know you did it! There, see, the lights are still on at the villa," Carrie cried triumphantly as she rounded towards the door and saw the lighted villa shimmering in the distance.

"Amazing."

The tone of his voice made her skin crawl. The gravel crunched as he moved towards her. "Don't touch me," Carrie hissed into the blackness.

"Come, we don't need light."

Carrie screamed as loud as she could and she ran from the room. As she raced along the rocky paths she tripped over a coiled garden hose and fell headlong against the plant tables. In a moment Bruno was at her side, where he solicitously enquired after her state of health as he raised her from the floor.

"Oh, you poor girl. Are you hurt?" he asked, pulling her towards him.

"Let me go."

"Come now, don't play games with me, Carrie. We both know why you came here tonight."

"*I* came here to see the flower you named after me," she exploded indignantly as he caressed her arm. "Now I know what *you* came for."

"Exactly. But don't sound so bitter about it. That attitude's so unbecoming to a lovely girl," he snapped as he knelt beside her.

In a wild effort to evade him, Carrie threshed about on the ground where the crushed rocks bit sharply into her skin. Futilely she bumped her legs beneath the plant table until eventually her feet became enmeshed in the snakelike garden hose. The more she tried to kick herself free, the more the hose seemed to uncoil.

Bruno was highly amused by her efforts. "Bravo, you're putting on a magnificent show." And he chuckled as he rocked back on his haunches.

"It's not a show," Carrie yelled as she managed to kick the hose aside.

"I think it's high time we stopped playing and got down to the serious business, don't you?"

His chilling words frightened Carrie, until she found the pulse choking in her throat. She valiantly struggled to free herself from his grasp, but Bruno seemed to be everywhere at once: his arms, his legs, his hands, all imprisoned her, painfully pressing her into the gravel path. Now a flood of water was oozing around her body and when she kicked out a clanking sound told her they had upset a watering can.

Bruno found the wetness equally disagreeable and he swore softly under his breath. "Enough! Do you hear me? Enough!" he growled at her.

Carrie yelped in surprise as she was slapped

across the cheek. Bruno's good humor had finally worn thin. What at first had seemed to be a novel overture to a seduction, had palled until his amusement had rapidly changed to anger.

"Please, I don't want to..." Carrie's protest was drowned by the smothering pressure of Bruno's mouth on her own as he pushed her to the floor. Vainly she struggled to throw off his weight, surprised by his unexpected strength.

"I told you that was enough," he growled viciously as he grabbed a handful of Carrie's hair to keep her head from bobbing about.

Suddenly the room exploded in light as a voice said:

"Yes, I agree, it's more than enough."

Carrie gasped in relief when she recognized the voice. "Tristano," she cried as she wriggled free of the Prince's arms.

Bruno crouched there, blinking stupidly in the light, unable to comprehend what had happened. "Cavalli?" he mumbled at last when he gathered his wits.

"That's right, and I ought to try to punch some sense into you, Bruno, but I'm afraid I'd be wasting my time."

Tristano stepped from behind a bank of concealing ferns, his face a mask of anger.

"Oh, how did you know?" Carrie gasped,

fighting tears of relief.

"Never mind *how* I knew, just consider it fortunate for you that I did know."

As the minutes passed Bruno quickly regained his usual suave manner. He slowly got to his feet and casually brushed bits of foliage and red dust from his cream gaberdine slacks. "Well, I can't exactly say you're welcome, Cavalli."

"You don't surprise me there," Tristano remarked dryly. "Are you all right, Carrie?" he asked, turning towards her.

"Yes, thanks to you," she whispered. She felt horribly ashamed to have to admit she had been very foolish. To have Tristano catch her in such an incriminating position was the worst discomfort of all. He avoided her eyes and she was glad, for it took more courage at this moment than Carrie possessed to be able to look him straight in the eyes and not blush with shame.

"You'd better get back to the house and clean yourself up. You're a mess. As for you," Tristano spun about to face Bruno, his fists clenched at his sides. "You should be ashamed pretending to name a flower after her just so you could get her out here alone. How did you come up with that pathetic line?"

At least Bruno had the decency to look

184

nonplussed by Tristano's scathing remark. "It wasn't a lie. You can see the orchid for yourself," he countered as he attempted to regain his dignity.

"No thanks, an evening tour of the gazebo doesn't appeal to me."

Again Bruno showed his discomfiture. He was at a loss to know where Tristano had gained his information, for he was sure Carrie would not have revealed their secret meeting to him. Smiling, he said, "Well, you're a veritable font of knowledge, my young friend. Do you have a crystal ball?"

Tristano ignored Bruno's attempts at humor. Instead he rounded on Carrie who was nursing her elbow as she leaned against the plant table listening to their exchange.

"I hope you're pleased with yourself, you little idiot. How many warnings do you need? After everything I had to say to you, to have accepted a suspicious invitation like this. I ought to..." Involuntarily his hand shot forward as he made a grab for Carrie's arm.

Alarmed by his angry face, Carrie leaped agilely away from him. "I already thanked you for your intervention. When I came out here I expected..."

"Don't stand there and lie to me by saying you intended to be part of a seduction. Do you take me for a fool?"

185

"Just leave me alone! My life's my own and I'll do what I want with it," Carrie cried, her legs going rigid with anger. "Will you never let up? You are still acting like some stupid guard dog, trailing me everywhere as if I was five years old."

"That's probably because you act as if you are five years old," Tristano retorted while his anger rasped in this throat as he fought to control his anger. "Now get back to the house like I told you. Or do you want me to carry you there like the baby you are?"

"Well, of all the nerve!" Carrie gasped in shock at the sheer anger radiating from his body. What should have become a lovely romantic interlude, wherein he wrapped her in his arms and told her how glad he was to have arrived in time to save her from Bruno's clutches, had turned sour. All Tristano intended to do was tell her how stupid she had been in between dishing out some new orders. Shaking his hand from her arm, Carrie bristled with anger. "Don't you dare tell me what to do," she cried, her face flaming with rage. "I'll go to the villa when I'm good and ready."

"Oh, is that so," he challenged, stepping towards her.

Carrie found her feet and on trembling legs, which felt as if they had been crushed in a vise, she ran for the gazebo door. Behind her she could hear Bruno's chuckles, followed by a scuffle and, a moment later, a dull thud as if someone had fallen. Carrie did not intend to wait to hear more. The men could settle their own differences without her. And lifting her wet skirts above her ankles, she ran outside into the black, windswept night.

The first raindrops, large as quarters, splashed against her face as she raced across the lawn. In deliberate defiance of Tristano's command, she ran the opposite direction to the villa. Carrie did not know where she ran, all she knew was that a tall black shadow was rapidly crossing the lawn to catch her. Gasping, gulping for breath, she increased her speed and she stumbled on the uneven ground. The rain was steadily increasing as the wind rose. Now her hair was whipped stingingly into her eyes, but she tossed it back without slackening her pace. The inky blackness of the lake loomed ahead through the gloom.

Pausing a moment to catch her breath, Carrie glanced behind her to find Tristano rapidly gaining on her. He was shouting something, but the wind was carrying his voice away. A flash of lightning crackled over the water to illuminate the surrounding countryside for a couple of moments as the sheet of brilliant light wavered and flickered through the surrounding hills. The lightning was followed by such a violent gust of wind, Carrie thought she would be picked up and swept out on the lake. By now the rain had increased to torrential proportions. Carrie hesitated a moment longer, realizing if she ran towards the lake she would be trapped. There was still time to change her course.

She turned a moment to check on her pursuer who was no longer visible in the driving rain, then she darted along the lake road towards the old monastery. There would surely be a place to hide from her pursuer in that jumble of vines and masonry. Though she loved him still, Carrie was suddenly afraid of Tristano's anger, which seemed to know no bounds in his zeal for controlling her actions.

All around her trees tossed violently, whipping and cracking with each frenzied gust. Huge black shadows raked the narrow path almost as if a living creature ran alongside her. Overhead the tall umbrella pines made a hissing sound in the wind. Cold rain, borne by a tearing wind, lashed her face as she ran into the full fury of the storm. The sheet lightning blazed above the trees once more, making Carrie gasp in surprise at the sudden blinding intensity of light. Then ahead, along the twisting path, she heard a

188

splintering sound above the wind. Too late, Carrie saw the splitting tree trunk as a fork of lightning shot and sputtered through the stand of trees to her left. A black shape flew before her, poised above her head for a terrifying instant, then crashed down. With a scream of horror, Carrie raised her arms in a vain effort to protect herself, but the falling tree limb knocked her to the ground where she sprawled in a heap on the rain soaked path.

A few minutes later Tristano reached the spot, his heart racing in horror as he beheld the form imprisoned beneath the splintered trunk. He knew it was Carrie from her light dress; besides, no one else would be foolish enough to be running through such a violent storm.

Kneeling beside her, he tried to lift the tree branch but the tangled smaller branches formed a dense brush. He found a second bough which he used as a lever to pry Carrie free. There she lay, unmoving on the ground, her long dress a pale blurr of sodden material. All about him the wind whirled and heavy thunder rolled across the lake, yet all Tristano could think about was Carrie's inert form and the reality of her danger. As he bent to scoop her in his arms, he muttered a prayer for her safety.

Running fleetly beneath the blazing

heavens, Tristano carried his burden home. Carrie's sodden skirts added to her weight, yet Tristano was surprised how easy it was to carry her; or perhaps the ease came from his own desperation which seemed to lend added strength to his arms as he stumbled along the slippery lakeside path. He had listened to her heartbeat and felt her pulse still beating weakly beneath his fingers. And he rejoiced in the proof she was still alive. The silent thanks he voiced for that miracle were the most meaningful prayer of his life.

Hoisting her higher and wadding her soaking skirts into a spiral about her slim legs, Tristano ran toward the lawn within sight of the villa. Except for a light in the hall, everywhere was in darkness. There was no telling where Bruno was. That blow on the jaw would only stun him for a few minutes, yet it was but a taste of what Tristano would have liked to give him. Just thinking about Bruno's sly scheming to lure Carrie to the gazebo on the pretext of admiring a flower he had named after her, made Tristano's blood boil.

At the villa's entrance he struggled to open the heavy teak door, and he carried his burden inside the darkened entrance hall. Everywhere appeared to be deserted. He yelled for someone to come to his assistance, but there was no reply.

Then, on the marble table inside the front door, he saw a folded paper. The *Principessa* had left a note for her husband. "I've gone with Gaby to Lena's party. Don't wait up. Maria and Juana have the night off – food in fridge. Sophia."

Scowling at the unwelcome news, Tristano pushed open the door of the first room leading off the grand circular hall. With his elbow he managed to switch on the light, then he staggered over to a yellow satin couch where he gently lowered Carrie onto the shining upholstery. Tristano stood back and flexed his tired arms, stretching, straining to relieve the ache in his muscles. That walk from the lake must have been at least two miles.

Now they were in the bright light he was able to examine Carrie's injuries more closely. How still she was! He was gripped with alarm at the sight of her colorless face and her sodden hair. With her dirty, rain-soaked garments, Carrie looked like someone rescued from the lake. For an instant the memory of that other time, years ago, when he had carried Marta to safety, shot through his brain. Impatiently he dashed the thoughts away. This was Carrie. And Carrie must live. He touched her head feeling through her thick wet hair for a lump where the tree trunk had struck her. He found it in a moment and he gasped at the size of the swelling which felt as large as an egg. The only first aid he could remember to ease her wound was the application of an ice pack.

On his way to the kitchens to get the ice pack, Tristano stopped at the liquor cabinet for a bottle of brandy. The liquor would bring much needed warmth to her chilled body. In the hallway he paused to use the phone. Though the violent storm would delay him, the doctor could still be here in less than an hour, yet by the look of that wan, corpse-like figure stretched lifelessly on the couch, an hour could be too long. Forcing himself to remain calm while he dialed the number, Tristano waited for a response. There was a series of clickings followed by an impatient "hello"; then the line went dead.

He cried aloud in his rage and disbelief. Then he hastily redialed the doctor's number. Now there was no sound on the phone. The storm must have brought down the lines. This often happened in this area, but of all the times for it to happen when Carrie desperately needed medical help.

After checking once more to see if she was still all right, Tristano went to the kitchens. Here everything was in darkness. He buzzed the bell for the housekeeper, hoping that perhaps she had returned early because of the storm, but there was no response. After a search he located a plastic bag and a towel to use as an ice pack. There was still no sign of the housekeeper when he made the return journey with the plastic bag stuffed with ice cubes from the refrigerator.

A deafening boom of thunder sounded directly overhead and the lights blinked once, then failed. Of all the luck! Not only were the phone lines down, but now the power was out.

Tristano went into the dining room hoping to find the candles which the *Principessa* had used at dinner. His luck held; here was the sconce where it had been left, a box of matches beside it.

When Tristano walked to Carrie's side holding the flaring candles aloft, the orange flames flickered in the wind casting grotesque shadows over the walls and furniture. The picture he made as he moved about the room made him think of some Victorian hero saving his ladylove from a fate worse than death. At the comparison Tristano smiled, but it was only a halfhearted attempt at humor. He placed several pillows beneath her head, and put the ice bag on the wound. Then when all was settled to his satisfaction, Tristano sat down to wait.

CHAPTER 9

When Carrie first opened her eyes, she thought she was blind, for no light, or shape, was visible.

There was a cloth dangling over her eyes. When she feebly reached up to move the obstruction, she found the movement caused such an excruciating pain in her head that she gasped with shock. Now the cloth was removed she could see, though it was not much improvement over total darkness. A mere pinpoint of light was visible; then, as her eyes focused, she watched the pinpoint become an oval candle flame. The flame gradually became two as her vision fully returned and her eyes grew accustomed to the strange light.

"Where am I?" she mumbled weakly, struggling to sit. Something cold and wet plopped from her head to her arm and she gasped in fright. It was only an ice pack. Gingerly Carrie explored the frigid patch on her head to discover a huge lump which was almost too painful to touch. The room had finally come into focus and she found it was not really as dark as she had thought at first. The twin candles added sufficient light to distinguish objects. On waking she had not remembered being in the Di Monde villa, but now she recognized the elegant antique furnishings and the deep fringed velvet curtains at the windows.

A sheet of lightning flashed beyond the tall windows, making her gasp a moment in shock. This sudden burst of light also alerted a second person in the room and she watched a man stagger from a winged chair beside the windows. In alarm Carrie wondered if it was Bruno. All the unpleasant incidents of tonight gradually began to return; she remembered Bruno and his attempted conquest in the flower filled gazebo. Though it hurt her head when she tried to remember, Carrie forced herself to recreate the fragments of events after she was presented with the Carrie orchid. Someone had come inside the darkened gazebo and turned on the lights, thereby ending her struggle with the Prince. Oh, how stupid, how foolish, she had felt lying there in the puddle of water from the overturned watering can, with her hair and dress soiled with greenery off the greenhouse floor. Then Tristano had said – Tristano!

The tall black shape was advancing on the couch and now, in the candlelit room, she could see the menacing stranger was Tristano.

Yet when he reached the couch, instead of heatedly denouncing her foolish actions as she expected, he knelt at her side. "Carrie, you're awake," he said.

"Yes. What happened?"

"Oh, *Dio*. I thought you were . . . well, never mind what I thought. How do you feel?"

"Groggy. And my head feels like it was trampled by a herd of buffalo. What happened?"

"Don't you remember?"

"I remember you coming to the greenhouse." Carrie shook her head. Some other pictures were gradually drifting back through the fogginess of her mind, vivid memories of flight and fear as she raced through drenching rain towards the lake. "You were chasing me towards the lake then I remember a falling branch . . ."

"The tree which gave you your headache. At first I thought maybe you were . . ."

"Dead," she supplied with a gasp and she shuddered as she voiced the word. Though she did not ask him, Carrie wondered what Tristano's reaction had been when that idea had registered. Had he felt pain, or any sense of loss, or had he merely muttered to himself in aggravation over her continuing stupidity? Though she desperately wanted to know the answer, Carrie was too afraid of the truth to ask.

"I tried to call the doctor, but the phone's out."

"What happened to the lights?"

"Out too. I was on my way back with the ice when everything went black. Luckily the *Principessa* was romantic enough to have candles at dinner, or we'd still be groping round in the dark."

He gently assisted Carrie as she struggled to a sitting position, clutching the soggy ice pack on her head as she moved.

"Here, I've got some brandy. Take a sip. It'll help," he suggested, holding a small glass to her lips.

Carrie sipped the fiery liquid and it made her cough.

"Ugh! It's terrible!"

Tristano laughed at her expression. "Thank God the *Principessa* isn't here to hear you say that about her best brandy."

"Isn't she here?" Carrie asked in surprise. Though she realized Tristano was not Bruno, there was still too much involvement between them for her to be spending the night alone with him, despite her incapacity.

"No, she's gone to a party with . . ." Tristano paused, deciding against mentioning Gabriella, "with friends," he concluded.

"Are they going to be back soon?"

He shrugged. "The storm will delay them, I'm sure. She may even spend the night. Are you afraid I'm going to pick up where Bruno left off?" he asked, amusement clear in his voice.

Carrie found she was reluctant to admit that was exactly what she had been wondering. "Oh, I guess you're safe enough. I suppose with the way you feel about me I'm assured of that," she said, finding the admission a painful one to make. Tears hovering close to the surface threatened to erupt until she managed to sniff them back as she forced herself to be calm.

"How can you know how I feel about you?" Tristano demanded, his voice going tense with anger.

"Please, I really don't feel up to arguing. I don't think I'd give a very good account of myself at the moment," she whispered, clenching her hands in her lap. How she wished the lights would come on or the *Principessa* come home, anything to keep her from having to spend the next few hours with Tristano Cavalli.

"Who said I wanted to argue," he muttered almost to himself. With that Tristano marched purposely to the window where he noisily drew the heavy velvet drapes to shut out the flaring picture of the storm.

"Is Bruno here too?" Carrie asked, desperate to make conversation, though she actually cared little for Bruno's whereabouts.

"Who knows? He's probably slinking away somewhere drowning his sorrows. Maybe he has another little girl who can be flattered by the promise of a flower named after her," he added, then he was ashamed of his taunt. "Sorry, forget I said that. If I'd had my way, Bruno would be unable to move."

"Didn't I hear you hit him?"

"Right, but it was only a pat. Now, if I'd given him what I've been saving for so long – *Dio*, he'd really be finished.

"I know it sounds dumb, but I really did think he was going to show me the greenhouse."

Tristano smiled sarcastically. "Oh, come now, don't tell me you had no idea what a perfect spot the gazebo made. You aren't still going to keep up that silly pretense, are you? For some reason – maybe his attention flattered you – you deliberately led Bruno on. It would have been a simple task in the beginning just to tell him to 'get lost' as you Americans say. No, Carrie, I'm afraid I can't believe it was all in good faith. You had an inkling at least, about Bruno's nefarious intentions.

199

Anger and humiliation made her face flush. Of all the nerve! How superior he sounded. "Why not? You of all people should know how I feel about casual affairs."

"Don't remind me." He pulled a face. "Perhaps you find a prince's attentions more appealing than mine. After all, he is a master of the art of seduction."

"And I suppose you aren't," Carrie snapped back, while she defensively clutched her melting ice pack.

Tristano smiled and shrugged at her statement. "Or so you seem to think."

"What else could I think after the way . . ."

"Couldn't you just settle for the fact that I find you attractive?"

Mutely Carrie stared at his shadowed face while she desperately wished their relationship could run as smoothly as his love affair with Gabriella appeared to do. They never quarrelled, despite Gabriella's sometimes possessive attitude; they laughed together; they kissed so romantically. All she ever seemed to do was quarrel with him. Self-pity washed over Carrie and hot tears flooded her eyes. If only she could go back to that first wonderful day in Venice, when he had been so admiringly attentive, instead of the way he acted toward her now. Sarcasm and hostility set the tone for their meetings.

Her tears threatened to spill over and in panic, Carrie staggered to her feet.

"I'm going up to my room," she said, ignoring the frown of disapproval which creased his brow. "I'll be more comfortable by myself. That way you won't have to put up with me." For a moment she wavered in the darkened room while she tried to gather strength for the arduous walk upstairs.

"You'll do nothing of the sort. The house is in darkness. Besides, you'll never make it up the stairs. Sit down!"

His gruff command had its usual effect. Seething with resentment at being ordered about, Carrie found the needed strength as she stepped around the marble-topped coffee table. "Will you stop giving me orders. I'm not your sister," she cried, glaring at him. Then as she took another step, her legs buckled and she clutched wildly at the marble-topped table to steady herself. For some indefinable reason the lighted sconce had begun to dance a wild fandango, and the room itself was echoing with a roar like a freight train hurtling along the tracks . . .

"Carrie!" Tristano's voice sounded weakly through the din before fading away as the floor came up to meet her.

He leaped to her side, muttering about her stupidity to hide his deep concern. She had fallen too quickly for him to save her. For the second time that night he picked her up and held her gently in his arms while he walked to the couch; as he laid her down, the power came on.

"Can you hear me, *Cara*," he whispered, lifting strands of hair out of her eyes.

Carrie did not reply. There was a hard lump framed by a red and purple bruise on her right temple. When she fell Carrie must have struck her head against the marble table. A second blow so soon after the first could prove to be extremely dangerous. Though her breathing appeared to be normal, Carrie's face was colorless, and there was a clammy film of sweat on her brow. Torn between the danger of leaving her alone, and the chance that the phones had also been repaired, Tristano decided to gamble on calling the doctor.

To his immense relief, when he picked up the receiver, there was a dialing tone. With shaking fingers, he dialed the doctor's number, but though he allowed the phone to ring for several minutes, there was no reply. This was the only doctor in the area, and even at that, he lived in the village on the other side of the lake. The only consolation was in his knowledge that the phones were working; at least he had a line of communication with the outside world. If necessary he could drive

Carrie to a hospital outside Venice.

When Tristano came back inside the room, Carrie was lying just as he had left her, limp as a rag doll on the bright yellow satin. For want of something to do, Tristano crossed to the bureau where he snuffed out the candles. Though throughout the ordeal he had steeled himself to remain calm, the sight of her lying there so white and still, sent a rapid surge of panic through him. At last he was forced to voice that inner dread which had haunted him ever since he had found her beneath the splintered tree. What if she died!

"Oh, *Cara*, no, I couldn't bear it," he whispered, going down on his knees beside her. Very gently Tristano gathered Carrie in his arms, cradling her head against his chest. For a few moments, which seemed to drag into eternity, there was no response until he pressed his lips against her cold face, while he whispered meaningless endearments in a desperate effort to arouse her from her unnatural sleep.

At first Carrie did not know where she was and there was still the roaring sound of a freight train in her ears, or perhaps that noise was the sound of the ocean? She felt warm and there was an indefinable sensation of well-being. Forcing her eyes open, which required a superhuman effort for the lids seemed to be glued shut, Carrie saw a room filled with bright light. There was someone beside her, holding her softly against his shoulder. It was a he, she decided, becoming aware of the masculine strength of those suntanned arms wrapped close around her. There was also a very pleasant masculine smell about the hot skin resting against her face. Though she knew she should have been alarmed to find herself in a stranger's arms, there was such an overwhelming feeling of safety about this stranger, that Carrie did not feel alarmed at all. In fact, she decided that she felt deliriously happy, despite the pain in her head.

"You are awake!"

Carrie stiffened as she recognized that husky voice. This, as all dreams must, had come to an end. Here she had been in such strong arms, basking in the heavenly feeling of being loved, thoroughly enjoying a newfound sense of security from the sensation, only to discover the new Prince Charming was none other than Tristano Cavalli.

"What happened?" she muttered as she struggled to be free of his arms.

Tristano allowed her to sit up. Despite the fact he did not mention it, he too had found their physical contact vastly rewarding; yet his worry over her safety had robbed the intimacy of some of its pleasure.

"You marched around the table and keeled over," he told her, his face forced into a grin, though he felt far from humorous. "How are you feeling?"

"Okay, I guess. Ouch!" Carrie found the fresh lump on her brow. "I see the lights came back on."

"Yes. And the phones are also working; unfortunately the doctor isn't home at the moment. No one else is here. Hey, what an idiot I've been. Lucia's next door. She can come over to help you. Would you like that?"

Carrie smiled her thanks. But when she swung her legs to the carpet as she prepared to get up, Tristano gently thrust her back.

"No. Perhaps now you'll listen to me. Stay where you are. You weren't steady enough to cross the room a few minutes ago, let alone go up three flights of stairs. At least now, though perhaps you still don't especially like me, you will at least give me credit for a minimum of intelligence."

Carrie's mouth trembled as she looked at his stormy face. No, she did not *like* him, she *loved* him. There was a vast difference between the two.

"Look, go call Lucia. I promise I won't move.

"Mind you keep your word," he warned

sternly as he walked from the room.

Carrie sat alone in the chill drawing room and she listened to him talking to someone over the phone. When Tristano came back inside the room he was smiling in relief.

"I don't know why I didn't think about Lucia before. You'll have to forgive me for being such an oaf."

Carrie had propped a heap of velvet pillows behind her back so she could sit up, and now Tristano viewed the arrangement with disapproval.

"You'd better lie down. People with head injuries are supposed to lie down."

"How do you know what they're supposed to do?" she challenged in a strained voice. Nevertheless, Carrie threw two of the pillows to the other end of the couch so that she was reclining rather than sitting. She did not want to reopen their quarrel. It had been so lovely just sitting here with his arms about her, even though at the time she had not known it was Tristano who held her close. That wonderful feeling of belonging had recreated all her fantasies concerning a strong man who could take care of her in any situation. Yet hadn't it been Tristano's fault she was in this situation in the first place? Had he not pursued her through the villa's grounds towards the lake, she would never have been hit by that falling limb.

"It doesn't matter what I do, you're determined not to give me credit for it, aren't you?" Tristano came to stand beside her, his face dark with anger. "Who brought you all this distance? Who carried you over two miles, mind you, through that tremendous storm? And who has stayed beside you up till now? Tell me that?"

Shamefaced, Carrie was forced to agree it was he. "Thanks for rescuing me. I really do appreciate it, you know I do."

Tristano spun on his heel and walked to the windows as a crunching sound came from the driveway. "Well, you certainly have a funny way of showing it," he snapped.

"I thanked you, what more do you want?" Carrie whispered, finding herself close to tears.

"What happened to civility? Couldn't we have one conversation without arguing? Couldn't you speak to me without snapping my head off?"

"I'm sorry if I've been snappy. I guess I'm not over that meeting in the fog when you went to such great pains to show me how gentle and persuasive you could be."

"How did you expect me to act when you ran away from me? Your anger and distrust were unwarranted."

"Oh, and I suppose the fact you're engaged to Gabriella shouldn't have been a deterrent to romance, huh? Well, let me tell you, Tristano Cavalli, I'm just not interested in a man who's already spoken for, not even on a casual basis."

"Look, I don't know where you get your information from, my dear *Signorina*, but I'm not 'spoken for' as you put it."

They faced each other; Carrie wan and tearful, though her anger was reviving beneath his angry glare; Tristano, his face growing as dark as the thunderstorm they had witnessed.

"Please, don't keep lying to me," Carrie whispered, gulping back the stupid tears that would not seem to stop. "The *Principessa* herself mentioned Gabriella was being fitted for a trousseau . . ."

"So what? That did not necessarily prove I have anything to do with it. There are thousands of Italian men who would be interested in marrying Gabriella. Her family is rich, she is titled, and she is also very lovely."

"Oh, how can you still pretend – how can you stand there like that and say those things to me . . ." Carrie could not go on for the lump in her throat threatened to choke her.

"Stand there and what?" Tristano yelled, then forcing his anger aside, he knelt beside her and took her small hands in his own. And though Carrie struggled to free his grasp, he would not let her break the bond between them. "No, you'll hear me once and for all. I'm not engaged to Gabriella. She happens to be someone else's bride-to-be, not mine. True, we've shared some years of close companionship, I won't lie about it." A smile lifted the corners of his mouth. "Let me say we'll always be friends, Gaby and I but nothing more."

Numbly Carrie heard his declaration. How much she wanted to believe him. How convincing he sounded. If she had not known he had to be lying, she would have believed him, for his handsome face bore such an earnest expression. And had she not known him better than he supposed, Tristano would probably have succeeded with his plan. The pressure of tears forming that solid lump of misery in her throat was almost unbearable.

"We'll probably be going home tomorrow, or the next day, so there's no need to pretend to me anymore."

"*Dio,* you are unbelievable. This is not pretense!" he cried in exasperation. "How can you accept gossip as fact when I've told you countless times it isn't true. Though you might think otherwise, I assure you I wouldn't go to such lengths to deceive an intended conquest. Don't you know I love you, you stupid girl!"

Carrie gasped at his heated declaration, her hand flying to her face in shock. Had she just imagined those words? Or had he really said he loved her? "You said . . . you said . . ."

"That I love you."

"But, what . . ."

If you say 'what about Gabriella', bump or no bump, I think I'll hit you," he said, his eyes flashing with temper.

There was a squeaking noise at the front door, followed by the click-clack of a woman's heels crossing the marble floor. Tristano spun toward the door to find his bewildered sister standing on the threshold.

"Ah, Lucia. Come in. I think she'll make it, but she's feeling pretty groggy still. Take a look at her. What do you think?"

Lucia casually dressed in jeans and a white sweater, ran towards the couch. "Oh, heavens, how did you get hurt, Carrie? Did you call the *dottore?*"

"Yes, an hour ago. I couldn't reach him. I'll go try again, perhaps he is home now."

Tristano left the room and Lucia came to Carrie and put her arms affectionately round her. Now, with the warmth of that sympathetic embrace, Carrie's hovering tears were released. Hugging Lucia as if she was her own sister, Carrie gave vent to her suppressed

210

grief as she buried her face on the other girl's soft cashmere covered shoulder.

"Shhh! Shh!" Lucia whispered in sympathy, holding her and rocking her like a baby. "I don't know why that stupid brother of mine didn't call me at first. But you know men! Come, it's all right now. You are safe."

After a few minutes more, Carrie felt relieved of the heavy sadness which had weighted her heart like lead.

When she saw that Carrie was through crying, Lucia smiled at her in genuine concern while she brushed Carrie's sticky, tangled hair from her brow. "There. I bet you're feeling better, eh! Men never understand about tears. Come, you must tell me all about it."

Carrie tried to explain how she came to be in her current predicament, delicately skirting around the incident in the gazebo which precipitated her accident. She need not have bothered to hide anything, for Lucia clucked and snorted appropriately over Bruno's shameful behavior.

"Oh, that one. He's gone too far this time," she cried indignantly.

Carrie felt very guilty about her part in Bruno's scheme. And she knew it would have been the honest thing to do to reveal to Lucia that she had suspected there was more involved in Bruno's invitation than an evening tour of the greenhouse. But if she told Tristano's sister that much, how could she explain her own acceptance of such terms. To tell her it had been done to anger her brother, or to make him jealous, would seem so childish and silly, she might lose Lucia's respect.

"He says he'll be here as soon as he can," Tristano voiced with relief as he strode back inside the room. "What a night not to be able to reach the doctor. How are you feeling now, Carrie? Does your head still ache?"

"I'll be okay," she whispered, meeting his eyes and seeing such genuine concern there she felt giddy with rekindled hope. Could she dare believe he was telling her the truth? Was there any chance that all those stories about Gabriella and Tristano were purely scandal sheet gossip after all. If only he had spoken the truth when he said Gabriella's trousseau was being gathered for her marriage with another man. Oh, how much she wanted to believe him, yet it was too much of an impossible dream to expect it to come true. If he spoke the truth and there was nothing between Gabriella and he, why was he always with her? What about that kiss during the dance, and the more passionate one shared outside in the moonlight? Those were not the actions of a woman engaged to another.

With Lucia's help, Carrie gingerly got to her feet. This time the room did not dance, nor was there that unpleasant roaring sound in her ears. After a walk about the room, Lucia made her sit down again. Tristano watched her progress, his face brooding, his eyes darkly unfathomable.

There came the crunch of tires on the driveway, and a car's headlights raked the silk paneled walls of the gold salon as someone drove up to the villa.

"Surely that can't be the doctor already," Tristano said in surprise. He went into the hallway to see who had driven up to the door.

Carrie smiled her thanks at Lucia while they waited. She could ask Tristano's sister about the validity of his story: Lucia had confided in her, so it would not be as if she had asked a stranger such a personal question.

"Lucia," Carrie began nervously while she twisted her hands together on her lap. "Will you answer an important question for me?"

"Of course, if I can," the other girl said, surprised that Carrie should hesitate to ask whatever she wanted to know. "What is it?"

"You know the Princess . . . Gabriella?"

"Of course, everyone knows Gaby."

"Does . . ." Carrie could hardly speak the words, because in all truth, she did not think she could bear to have the thin thread of her illusion permanently severed. "Does Tristano love her?"

Lucia shrugged. "Who knows? Does Tristano ever really 'love' a woman?"

The answer had been evasive. Carrie bit her lip as she contemplated asking another question. How much she dreaded hearing the truth. It did not matter that tomorrow she might be on her way home with no chance of ever meeting Tristano Cavalli again; if she went home with the merest doubt that he had not lied when he said he loved her, she would never rest. Nor would she have peace of mind while she still wondered if he was even free to promise such a thing to her. "Is Tristano going to marry Gabriella?"

"I don't think so." And Lucia laughed at the suggestion.

Baffled by Lucia's behavior, Carrie was even more confused than she had been before she sought to learn the truth. "But isn't Gabriella going to be married? She's having a trousseau. Why else would that be necessary?"

Lucia shrugged at her question. "I think she intends to be married, but with Gabriella one never knows until she actually goes to the altar. This isn't the first time. She's been engaged a half dozen times before. Tristano says she has the mentality of a spoilt child."

At that moment the shrill tones of a familiar voice rang through the hallway. Carrie froze in her chair when she recognised the laughing, high-pitched tones. The visitor was Gabriella!

When footsteps sounded at the doorway, Lucia went to greet their visitor.

Well, she already had her answer, Carrie thought miserably, though Lucia had not definitely said the bridegroom was Tristano, the coupling of those two names should be proof enough. He had lied to her once again. After all those delicious last minute hopes it was terribly painful to admit she had been right in distrusting him all along. This was one time that being right was no reward at all. And Carrie felt like sinking through the floor. How could she face them both now, when she felt so hurt and deceived?

CHAPTER 10

"Well, so you are a maiden in distress," Gabriella cried in a voice bubbling over with laughter. "How much Tristano loves to play boy scout. I trust he's taken good care of you? What, *Caro,* no splint," she exclaimed with a wicked grin as she turned to face him.

"One does not put a splint on the head, Gaby."

"Oh, then that's the only reason she doesn't have one." Gabriella came to the couch where she smiled down at Carrie. "Do you feel terrible?" she asked.

Carrie nodded, surprised to hear the concern in Gabriella's voice. Her sympathy seemed genuine, and though she was glad of it, Carrie could not accept Gabriella's friendship now, not knowing what she knew about her commitment to Tristano. "I'll probably have the biggest headache of my life in the morning."

"Well, you've come to the right person. I have the most marvelous remedy for headaches. It's something my father used for hangovers. Tristano will have to get the recipe for you. I expect you'll be needing it," Gabriella said, after she had stooped over Carrie's face to study the extent of her injuries.

"That stupid Bruno's the cause of this," Lucia exploded, her dark eyes flashing with anger. "Wait till I see him, I'll give him a tongue lashing."

"It will be wasted, Cia. Bruno has a head like a donkey. I'm sure, when he's ninety years old, he'll still be chasing pretty women.

Or for that matter, perhaps anything in skirts. Poor Sophia, how does she stand him?"

Carrie squirmed in discomfort when she heard them discussing Bruno's well known failing. His philandering seemed to be such common knowledge, she felt highly embarrassed to have become even a small part of it. Tristano had been angered by her seemingly receptive mood toward Bruno's flirting, yet even that small triumph had a hollow feeling. There was no reward in rousing the jealousy of someone else's intended husband. Had Tristano been honest with her instead of telling all those wonderful lies about his feelings for her she would never have led Bruno on. Now she must live with the humiliation of having them laugh at her behind their backs for being such a gullible idiot. Carrie sniffed and made an effort to swallow her hurt pride. There was nothing for it now but to grin and bear it. The damage was already done. At least she would not have long to wait before Ed would be helping her load her luggage in to the taxi for the return flight home. Then, once she was thousands of miles away, she would be able to forget the handsome, fascinating rogue named Tristano Cavalli. Carrie's spirits were so low, that brave statement sounded exactly like the lie it was!

"Where's everybody?" Lucia asked, coming

to sit beside Carrie. And she patted her arm in sympathy.

"The *Principessa's* driving back. Oh, and *Signorina* Neal's business associates are with her. The party was a terrible failure. Lena was an absolute horror," Gabriella explained with a frown. "Sophia thought perhaps she'd be interested in some ideas the Americans had. You know she has a whole string of shabby villas across the lake; but no, they are to stay in absolute ruin rather than be developed. Some people have no initiative."

Tristano smiled at Gabriella's disclosure on business matters, which he found an unusual diversion for the lovely woman. Gabriella's mind generally hinged on nothing more serious than the next party and what she would wear to it.

"My goodness, how intellectual you are becoming. I fully expect to find you reading a book someday," he quipped sarcastically. And he winked at Carrie as he spoke.

Feeling uncomfortable, Carrie looked away quickly from the shared intimacy. It was too painful to endure after her recent discovery of his duplicity.

Gabriella laughed as she crossed to the cabinet to pour herself a drink. "Anyone else?" she asked, holding up a bottle of liquer.

"Make mine something a little stronger,"

said Tristano. "What about you, Lucia?"

"Nothing for me thanks."

Gabriella poured a drink and handed it to Tristano. As she passed him she gave him a light peck on the cheek and the sight of their easy affection was another stab in Carrie's heart.

"You are so sarcastic. Women should know things about business matters. I intend to learn about the family business. In fact, I'm going to become so clever, you'll hardly know me." And Gabriella laughed in delight when she saw Tristano's shock. "I knew you'd be surprised by that. Women can't always stay under the thumb of you men. There's a whole world out there waiting for us. Am I not right, Carrie?"

Carrie forced a smile of agreement. For once she found Gabriella making a genuine effort at friendship, yet this was not the time for it. She was no longer able to respond in a friendly manner to Gabriella, for inside her heart she nursed a tender wound. How lovely Gabriella looked, even at this hour with the devastation of the storm apparent on her expensive clothing. Her amber dress was spotted with rain, and her slender, nylon-stockinged legs were all splattered with mud. There was nothing Gabriella could do to make herself appear unsightly, Carrie was convinced of this; perhaps she would be lovely first thing in the morning too, every inch a princess. And the reminder that Tristano would know firsthand the truth of that assumption, twisted the pain a little deeper.

"Tristano doesn't share your views, Gaby," Lucia joined, a fighting gleam in her dark eyes.

"My dear, I heard about that. He's really very naughty... You should be ashamed, Tristano," Gabriella clucked, stroking his cheek with her long white hand with its perfectly manicured fingernails of pearly pink. "Very naughty indeed."

He grinned and turned away. "Now I'm not going to take on three females. Carrie's already had a go at me over the job, Lucia. I see you've recruited Gaby as well.

"Wrong, you dreadful ogre. The ideas are all my own," Gabriella quickly explained. "I think Cia should have a chance to prove herself in a job if she wishes. *Gioia* is a very respectable publication. Heavens, if it weren't, I'd never have appeared in it," she added in indignant tones.

Her statement made both Lucia and Tristano laugh.

"You'll keep on at me until I either crack, or give in, I can see," he said in amusement as he went to the cabinet for a refill. While

Tristano poured a drink he asked, "What about you, Carrie? Did I convince you to mind your own business?"

Not sure if he was serious or joking Carrie said, "If I believe in something I never give up."

Gabriella laughed in delight at her answer. "There, you see! Oh, I can see Aldo is going to have an easy time of it in persuading you to allow Cia to take the job. We three will lend our support. Perhaps we can get the *Pincipessa* on our side, too," Gabriella suggested with a wicked gleam in her eyes. "There's charm in numbers."

"Is Aldo coming over then?" Tristano asked in surprise.

"Yes, he's with the *Principessa*. The wedding's so close now, he's going to practically live on the doorsteps till it's over."

"Here comes a car now. I hope that's the doctor."

After Tristano went to the door to admit the new arrival, Carrie stared miserably at the patterned gold carpet under her feet. Lucia and Gabriella were talking to each other in Italian and she felt terribly excluded. Once more there had been the mention of Gabriella's forthcoming marriage, as if she needed any more hints.

"Here she is," Tristano said to a tubby,

221

middle-aged man in a black raincoat who was walking beside him.

"Ah, this *Signorina* doesn't need me. She looks so well already. And I thought you were at death's door, my dear, but here you are, sitting up and looking lovely."

Carrie managed a wan smile at the doctor's compliments, though she felt more like bursting into tears. Tonight had been too much and she could not wait for the privacy of her own room where she knew she would succumb to a flood of self pity. The emotional drain of the past hours had left her feeling exhausted.

After a swift examination during which he peered at the bumps on her head and shone a bright light into her eyes, the doctor assured Tristano that his guest would survive.

"Yes, she's going to be fine. But I'll leave a sedative, just in case," the doctor decided as he reached inside his black medical bag.

The sound of numerous voices drawing closer alerted them all to the arrival of the *Principessa's* party at last. Carrie knew there would be some explaining to do now that Ed was here.

"Oh, you poor girl. What a terrible accident," the *Principessa* cried when she was informed of the situation. She came to Carrie and gave her a sympathetic kiss on the cheek.

The soft folds of the *Principessa's* green silk gown exuded an aura of expensive perfume. "The servants aren't back yet, I suppose. Perhaps I can cook something myself. I used to cook in the old days, believe it or not. How about a bowl of soup. Would you like that?"

"It's very kind of you, but I really don't need anything to eat," Carrie protested. "You mustn't go to any trouble for me." She felt especially guilty now the *Principessa* was offering to cook for her when it was through her own foolishness with the *Principessa's* husband that she had been brought to this circumstance in the first place.

"It's no trouble at all. In fact, it'll be great fun. Come with me, Gaby, it's high time you at least learned to boil water."

Gabriella pulled a face, but she followed the *Principessa* obediently to the kitchen. Ed and Tim were hovering in the background, asking Carrie a million questions and both looking very worried about her health, although the Italian doctor assured them their friend would probably feel better after a night's sleep. The question of flying home within the next couple of days was something else: the doctor said he would make no decision until he had examined Carrie again in the morning.

Another man had come inside the room with the others, someone Carrie had not met before. He had smiled sympathetically at her before devoting his entire attention to Gabriella. That was only to be expected. As he would hardly make a pass at Lucia while her brother was in the room, that left the lovely Gabriella as prime target. Yet surprisingly, though the man slid his arm familiarly around Gabriella's slim waist. Tristano had not seemed to be offended by his action. Carrie was frankly puzzled by the social mores of the Italian upper class. She was convinced she would never sort them out if she lived here a year.

"Carrie, I want you to meet someone," Tristano said, coming towards her. the stranger was following him.

Carrie smiled politely at the gray-haired man who was in his fifties. He was very distinguished looking in his expertly cut gray suit with a silk shirt and tie. And he was also very rich; Carrie could tell this by his expensive clothing and the flashing rings on his slender hands. It figured: only a rich man would be given the time of day in a home like this. She, Ed and Tim were only here by the skin of their teeth and as business associates they did not really fit in with the glamorous occupants of luxury villas.

"Here, I know you'll want to meet this very important gentleman." Tristano smiled as he stood aside to allow the stranger to greet her.

"I am charmed to make your acquaintance," the man said in a harsh, heavily accented voice. "Allow me to introduce myself, *Signorina*. I am Aldo Neri, the publisher of *Gioia Fashion Magazine*."

"I'm very pleased to meet you. I'm Carrie Neal. Aren't you the man who wants to give Lucia a job?"

"That's right. I hear you're very much in favor of the move."

"Yes. I work because I have to, but even though Lucia does not need to support herself, I think she deserves a chance to be her own person."

Aldo Neri smiled at her statement. "You are a very wise lady. What do you think, Tristano?"

"Oh, yes, she's wise. She also thinks I'm a male chauvinist, or whatever they are called."

Aldo Neri laughed. "She is not only wise, but she's also observant, my friend."

Tristano grinned in face of the opposition from all sides.

"You are all making it very difficult for me to say no."

"Perhaps you should say yes instead," Lucia interrupted, coming over to Aldo and linking her arm in his. "Thank you, anyway," she whispered.

225

"Carrie, do you think I should agree to let Lucia have a trial period at the magazine?" Tristano asked, his face serious.

Carrie gasped in surprise, hardly expecting the question. "Sure. I think that's a wonderful idea."

Lucia's face was wreathed in smiles and she hugged Carrie first, then came over to give Tristano a kiss of thanks. "Oh, thank you, you adorable male chauvinist. You'll see, I can make you proud of me."

Tristano patted her affectionately and ruffled her hair. "It's not usual for me to bow to opposition. I must be getting soft in my old age."

At that moment the *Principessa* walked inside the room carrying a large tray with glasses and bowls of steaming soup. Gabriella followed her with a plate of buttered bread and a platter of fruit.

"Here we are, everyone, come and eat. It's simple and fixed by my own hand. Not very many people can say they've eaten food prepared by the *Pincipessa* di Monde." When the round of laughter had subsided, she glanced about the room in surprise. "Isn't Bruno here yet? I was sure he'd have been down after all this commotion."

Those who were acquainted with the full story about tonight's events glanced at each

226

other for a moment of discomfort, before Tristano stepped forward with a smile. "Oh, I forgot to tell you, he's over at my place."

The *Principessa* smiled at him as she turned her attention to serving the impromptu meal. "He'll miss my cooking then, won't he?" she said.

Carrie, watching from the sidelines, thought she saw the *Principessa's* mouth tighten for a moment before she resumed her practised smile. And she felt sorry for her, for she suspected the *Principessa* had guessed the story behind her accident and if not that much, then at least she knew Tristano had lied to save her from embarrassment.

While she watched everyone milling about while they took what food they wanted and accepted drinks from Aldo Neri, who was acting as bartender, Carrie felt a stab of pain. Why should Tristano not tell a convincing lie, he apparently made such a habit of lying his way out of difficult situations. It was foolish of her to be surprised.

The soup had become unappetizing now, and the bread was tasteless. Carrie could only stare miserably at her plate without really seeing it. Though everyone tried to be kind to her, they often lapsed into Italian, thus excluding her from the conversation. She glanced across the room to where Tim and

Ed perched on a narrow petit point covered bench and they exchanged sympathetic smiles with her. This made Carrie feel much better. Once she was on the plane she would forget Tristano, Gabriella and the Prince and the *Principessa* di Monde. No longer would they be a part of her life. All this would be like a bad dream.

"Hello, *Cara*, you must eat your soup. It will make you feel much better."

Carrie bit down on the spoon as she found Tristano standing beside her. She grew even more uncomfortable as he prepared to share the couch with her.

"Oh, I'm not really hungry," she whispered, avoiding his deep brown eyes.

Not wholly satisfied with her answer, he reached out to tilt her chin, until she was looking directly at him. "Hey, what's the matter now?"

"The same thing that was the matter before," she said sharply, turning her head away.

"But I . . ." Tristano stopped, realizing as far as Carrie was concerned nothing had changed. "Wait, we'll soon alter that woebegone face."

"*Dottore*, have you met *Signor* Neri?" Tristano asked as he approached the doctor who was trying to munch his way through a slice of buttered bread which had been pressed on him by the *Principessa,* while in his other hand he juggled a wineglass and a slice of gateau. "Here, let me take those," Tristano offered as he helped him to a chair.

"Thank you," the doctor said as Tristano brought him a plate. "I'm not used to this cocktail party eating." Now the doctor felt more secure with a plate for everything. "No, I haven't met him, but I overheard him introduce himself to the young patient. Is he a new resident of the area?"

"No, not yet, but he soon will be." Tristano looked back to Carrie, a gleam of triumph lighting his dark eyes. He was deliberately speaking in English for her benefit. "Aldo is going to be Gabriella's husband."

"Oh, I must congratulate him then," the doctor said, pleased and surprised by the unexpected news. "But I always thought it was you were going to claim the lovely lady."

Tristano smiled and shook his head. "No, I'm going to choose someone quite different from Gaby for my wife."

Carrie had heard their exchange as she was meant to do. Surely Tristano would not go to such lengths to live a lie. When Gabriella accepted the doctor's congratulations which was celebrated with a toast to the happy couple, Carrie still could not believe her ears.

She must be dreaming! Could it be possible Tristano had spoken the truth when he said he loved her? She stopped chewing, wadding the piece of bread into an unpalatable lump against the roof of her mouth. Had she really heard what she thought she had heard? The middle-aged stranger who was to be Lucia's employer was also to be Gabriella's husband!

"Now, you little doubting Thomas, what do you say to that?" Tristano asked at last when he seized her half-empty plate and put it on the table. "Well, say something. Surely you're pleased to hear the news. Or at least tell me you believe me now. I assure you, all the people in this room haven't been bribed to go along with a lie. Aldo and Gaby are to be married next month, and though their engagement has been an on again, off again, affair, Gaby assures me it is definitely *on*. Aldo is very rich," Tristano confided in an undertone, "far richer than I. And if there's anything Gaby loves, it's a rich man. Money can provide everything in life she deems essential – luxury, travel, clothes, high living. Aldo will provide it all."

"I almost can't believe it's true," Carrie gasped, as she turned to face him and read the truth of his words in his face. Tristano smiled softly at her as he touched her face, his fingers gentle against her skin.

"You can believe it, *Cara*. You can also believe everything I've ever told you about the depth of my feelings for you."

"You really . . ."

"Love you. Yes, very much and I want you to be my wife."

Carrie gulped at the stunning words. Everywhere spun crazily around in a carousel of noise and light. She felt Tristano's strong arm come out to steady her and she rested her head against his shoulder where she uttered a sigh of complete satisfaction. All those wonderful feelings she had cherished during her waking moments earlier this evening were going to begin again. This time it was real; no longer a fantasy which faded with the light. Tristano loved her. He wanted her to be his wife. And though she still could not adjust her thinking to include the latter, the former declaration was intoxicating enough.

"Shall we tell the others? You know people always say good things come in pairs," Tristano whispered, as his arm slid around her shoulders.

"Can we tell Ed and Tim first," Carrie ventured, nervously glancing at the other beautiful, poised people in the room. If Tristano made her his wife she would have to socialize with these people. She would be required to play the hostess to princes and *principessas,* to counts . . .

"What's the matter?" Tristano asked, noticing her paling face. "Aren't you feeling well? Are you going to pass out on me again?"

Carrie shook her head. When she reached for his hand he gripped her fingers so reassuringly, she felt a little of her apprehension lessening at the contact. "How can I compete with people like Gabriella? Even Lucia is used to living in palaces and attending grand balls. I come from a small frame house in a provincial town and our biggest entertainment in an evening is watching TV. I don't think I can do it, Tristano, I wouldn't know what knives and forks went at the table, or how to talk to princes and princesses."

"Don't be silly. You can't fob me off with a flimsy excuse like that." Tristano laughed, gathering her to him in a joyful embrace. "The servants will set the tables and I will teach you the correct form of address. Besides, you've been living here with a prince and princess. They aren't any different from other people, are they?"

Carrie shook her head, allowing herself to relax against his side. "No, I guess not. I just wanted to let you know so you wouldn't expect too much from me. My social training is limited to church socials and cafeterias."

Tristano was laughing again and the others turned to see what he found so amusing. "All right, everybody, I've an annoucement to make too," he cried, immediately gaining their attention. "First we must drink a toast to Gabriella and Aldo, then we will drink a second toast to me."

"You!" Gabriella exploded in mirth. "Now why should we drink a toast to you? Being a boy scout doesn't merit a toast."

His eyes sparkling with the excitement of his news, Tristano took a deep breath, and he waited a moment before continuing. "I'm going to be married too!"

Gabriella's eyes narrowed at the news, then she caught Aldo watching her and she forced a polite smile to her perfect mouth. "You! Why, surely not the world's most confirmed bachelor! Who is the lucky, or should I say, *unlucky* . . ."

"Don't be such a cat," Lucia interrupted.

Gabriella laughed at Lucia's observation, but her face flushed slightly beneath its perfect makeup. "Tell us who she is."

Tristano took Carrie's hand and raised her to her feet. "Here she is. Hadn't any of you guessed?"

From somewhere near at hand Carrie heard the tinkling crash of breaking glass. At the shocking announcement Tim had dropped his drink while Ed just stared at her, his pipe drooping from the corner of his mouth in such a comical pose, Carrie had to fight the impulse to laugh.

"Carrie," Ed managed at last, his voice creaking.

"Yes, I know it's sudden, but I'm a man who makes up his mind quickly. You should know that, *Signor* Stern. As you are Carrie's guardian in a sense while she is here in Venice, I hope we have your approval."

Ed gulped and cleared his throat. "Well, I'm not really in charge of her. Carrie's old enough to make up her own mind about things."

"What a lovely surprise," the *Principessa* cried, coming to the rescue as she grew anxious to smooth over the obvious amazement reflected in the Americans' faces. Tristano had always been impulsive, so his unexpected announcement was not as earth shattering to her as it was to the other guests. "Carrie, how nice. Now we shall be neighbors," the *Principessa* said, coming to hug Carrie to her. She remarked on the dampness of her dress. "Oh, my dear, come, let's change your gown. You'll catch your death of cold. Tristano, you should be ashamed, you could at least have brought her a blanket. I had no idea how wet she was,"

234

she scolded as she swept Carrie out of the room away from the shocked glances of her compatriots and Gabriella's barely concealed jealousy. Only Lucia seemed to accept and rejoice in her brother's choice.

"I wanted to talk to you alone," the *Principessa* confided, as they walked slowly up the broad flight of stairs.

"About what?" Carrie questioned, wondering uneasily if the *Principessa* was going to try to talk her out of her decision.

"Now don't sound so apprehensive. First let me say how much I'm in favor of the match. When Tristano makes up his mind, it's for all time. I know him like my own son, as indeed he almost was, in a manner of speaking."

Carrie's discomfort increased at the reminder that Tristano had been engaged to the *Principessa's* daughter; but the soft, cool hand on her arm imparted understanding, not hostility. "Yes, he told me about Marta," she revealed, wondering how she should refer to the dead girl.

"Yes, they were to be married. Although, at the time, I wondered if Tristano knew what responsibilities being married entailed. It's very difficult for a wife when the man retains his adolescent..." the *Principessa* paused, glancing toward Carrie and seeing her face

235

flushed with discomfort. "No, I don't blame you. I suspected you wanted to spur Tristano to jealousy by it. And Bruno is very easy to encourage. That, after all, is an acceptable way for a woman to bring a man to his senses. Bruno intended to use you, but the tables were reversed this time. In the beginning I thought about warning you, but I was afraid you wouldn't take my interference kindly. So, I had to allow things to take their course. Though I must admit, I didn't expect you to be hit on the head in the process."

They had reached the *Principessa's* door and she admitted Carrie to a beautifully appointed room decorated in turquoise and gold. Vast swatches of fabric were looped about the windows which stood open to the rain. The *Principessa* clucked in disapproval as she discovered the window catch had come unfastened.

"Sit down. I'll only be a minute," she called over her shoulder, as she struggled with the window. Satisfied the catch was secure, she came towards the bed where Carrie was perched. "Because my girl was to marry Tristano I feel somewhat different towards you, it's only natural. But I don't think my feelings are bad, on the contrary. Tristano has no mother, and, as your own will be so far away, I'd feel honored if you would allow me to take the place of a mother-in-law."

Carrie's eyes had widened in surprise at the suggestion; thankfully she accepted the *Principessa's* cool hand as she came to sit beside her on the gold satin coverlet. "Having you next door will be like having my Marta back again. Oh, Lucia is sweet and lovely, and lovely Gaby is my god-daughter, but they're not like you. They are both a product of their class, self assured, restless . . . though you're a working girl, you have that charm which I naturally associate with the young. Once she passed fourteen, even my Marta had lost that. Oh, because I was her mother, I loved her, despite her faults. But lovely though she was, I know she would not have made Tristano happy. I think you will."

"Me! Really?" Carrie gasped.

The *Principessa's* laughter pealed out in delight at Carrie's genuine surprise. "Really. Ah, you are delightful. I think also that you will make me happy too."

Carrie was surprised once more when the *Principessa* clasped her in a light embrace. Then she got up and went to the deep built-in cupboards lining the opposite wall.

"Come, we must dress you in something dry or everyone will think we were up to something, won't they."

After rummaging through the garments the

Principessa extracted a long crimson brocade robe trimmed in gold. "Here, this should fit you."

Carrie exclaimed over the luxurious garment and she pulled off her soiled dress and slid her arms inside the heavy brocade sleeves. In this garment she too felt like a princess. "Thanks. It's really lovely, but you didn't have to do this."

"Oh, yes I did. Now I have a favor to ask of you."

"A favor? What favor can I do for you?"

The *Principessa* went to another wardrobe and took out a long white dress shrouded in a plastic dress cover. She carefully lifted off the shield to reveal a billowing, fulltrained creation of white silk trimmed with lace and knots of rosebuds. Carrie gasped in delight at the sumptuous garment.

"Ah, I can see you like it too."

"Oh, it's lovely! Is it a wedding dress?"

"Yes. A lovely, old, handmade dress. It belonged to Tristano's mother and her mother before her."

Carrie was almost afraid to touch the exquisite folds of fabric as she lifted a handful of silk to admire the hand embroidered panels beneath the knots of rosebuds.

"It's lovely. Are you keeping it for Lucia?"

"Yes, she'll wear it if she can fit in it. I don't

know about Lucia, with her, Sophia Loren is not in it, eh!" the *Principessa* chuckled at her own thoughts. "I have it here at the villa because Marta wished to wear it at her wedding. When she ... died," the *Principessa* paused, her mouth tightening as she continued, "there was no need for the gown. Tristano told me to keep it for him. As a matter of fact, I think he's forgotten it's here. Will you wear it for me, Carrie? And for him too. This dress is a tradition in the Cavalli family."

Carrie's eyes filled with tears and she squeezed the *Principessa's* hand. "Yes, I'll be honored to wear it. I never hoped to have such a lovely dress for my wedding day."

"Thank you, my dear." The *Principessa* returned the wedding dress to the wardrobe and she closed the door. "Come, they'll be missing us downstairs. I'm surprised Tristano hasn't come up to claim his bride. Perhaps the others won't let him go."

Carrie smiled at the *Principessa's* words as she agreed with her.

When they walked from the room they discovered Tristano just rounding the top of the stairs.

"What did I tell you? Here she is, all safe and sound."

Tristano smiled down at Carrie and slid his

239

arm around her waist. "Now I've found her, I don't want to lose her," he said to the *Principessa,* who had begun to walk back to her room.

"You two young ones go down together," she said, smiling at the attractive couple. "I don't want to spoil things. I'll come down in a little while." Then exchanging a secret smile with Carrie, she disappeared inside her room.

"Isn't this robe lovely? It belongs to the *Principessa,*" Carrie said, making small talk to hide her insecurity now she was alone with Tristano at last. "She wanted me to see your mother's wedding dress. She asked me to wear it at my wedding."

"Ah, so that was it. I should have suspected she was up to something cagey," he said with a slow caressing smile. "You will look exquisite in the gown. It will also make the *Principessa* very happy; she had such hopes of seeing the dress on her daughter, but she will be finally pleased to at least have a hand in helping me select a wife. She has taken the place of my mother, in a small way. I like her very much and I hope you do too."

"Oh, yes, very much."

Carrie's heart began to pound as Tristano drew her closer and locked his arms about her back. There was no more harmless talk to distract him, nobody to come flitting down

240

the corridor. They were all alone on the dark landing and she discovered she was still unsure of how she should act with him. They had spent too many hours quarreling for her to feel secure in his presence. What she wanted from him and what she had come to expect were not always the same.

"I don't know whether to kiss you, or slap you," Carrie said at last, as she finally gave in to the magic of his nearness and relaxed against his shoulder.

"If I've a choice I'd say the kiss. That would be so much pleasanter," he whispered, raising her head so he could look into her eyes. "Ah, *Cara*, at last I've found my perfect lady. Though all that time spent quarreling with you certainly undermined my confidence. There was a time when I wondered if we could ever face each other without the sparks flying. Say we'll never quarrel again. Say you won't slap me, or argue with me . . ."

"I can say it, but I might be lying," she whispered with disarming honesty. Then she slipped her hands up to his neck and fastened her fingers in his thick dark hair.

"No, not lies. We will always speak the truth to each other."

"That's fine with me."

"You still have something to tell me, you know."

"What is that?"

"You never formally accepted my marriage proposal."

"Oh, that." Carrie breathed a satisfied sigh as she raised her mouth for his kiss. "There was never any doubt that I'd accept once I was convinced you were free to marry me."

"Ha, that's your first lie. Now, hush, you talk too much, little American girl. I can see I'll have my work cut out to teach you to be a proper Italian wife."

Carrie kissed him back, and she gripped his wide shoulders drawing him closer until their bodies were pressed tightly together. Darkness swirled around her and the wind rustled the curtains at the windows as she sank into the heady sweetness of love which was hers at last. There was no other woman's shadow hovering in the background, no doubts about this man's promises. He was hers alone.

"There's no one I'd sooner have as my teacher," she breathed when their lips parted.

"Nor I as a pupil," Tristano said. And he bent his dark head to her fair one to cement his words with a kiss of love.